TALL TALES

FROM

AN ISLAND

By
Peter Macnab

Luath Press Ltd.,
Barr, Ayrshire.

First Edition, 1984

Other works by Peter Macnab include 'The Isle Of Mull'.

Leanaibh gu dluth ri cliu bhur Sinnsir

(Follow ye closely to the fame of your ancestors)

CONTENTS

INTRODUCTION

My father and grandfather were both Mull men, and the first twenty five years of my own life were spent in that island.   An old man once said to me: 'The older you get, the more your thoughts will turn to the place where you were a boy.'   How right he was!   Now that the years have dropped behind, like milestones along a fast country road, I think more and more about the island and its background.   In fact, my wife and I now live there for much of the year in our little house among the birch and hazel trees looking down to the narrow loch, at the head of which stands the little hamlet whose busy street is the subject of one of my stories.

I do believe that Mull, of all the islands, has the richest heritage of storytelling, an art handed down through the centuries by word of mouth from the *seannachies* of the ancient clans to the shepherd on the hill and the roadman in the quarry.   Youth is an impatient listener: when all the world was young, with the rivers, hills and woods to explore, games to play, and school as a grim distraction from such important pursuits, I found my boyish attention wandering when grown-ups began to talk round the fireside of the old things and the old ways.   Still, something of the atmosphere remained, and a few of the stories.   It was when I grew older that I became more interested in tales from the past, and in time I came to realise

I

that I was learning something of the romantic social history, not only of the island and its people (for the stories could well apply to any of the islands), but of the Highlands and Islands, remembering that in Europe their Celtic culture comes next in antiquity to those of Greece and Rome.

I began to analyse the background of some of the more obscure stories and found that in so many cases they are really founded on something tangible, the origin of which has been lost in the mists of time, and the stories altering slightly every time they were passed on from generation to generation until they have ended up in their present form. They will not change much from now on, though, because for the first time the songs and stories that still survive are being written down, and no longer rely on folk memory for their immortality.

For example, take the story of the cairns marking the leaps of the Gille Reoch. I examined the three cairns in their boggy hollow, probing deeply into their foundations with a thin iron rod. To judge from the depth to which the earlier stones had sunk, and been added to, they have been there for hundreds of years. Undoubtedly, the story of the athletic MacKinnon swordsman is founded on some such real incident far back, perhaps in the Middle Ages and recorded in stone for posterity. But it was also recorded in the tale itself, which has passed through a great many tellings, each of them slightly different from the last.

Of course, I must warn you that not all the stories fall into this category, and I leave it to the reader to judge which are based on facts, however tenuous, and which on fiction! Many of these Tales are no more than prime examples of the story-tellers' art, and none the worse for that. Some of the stories have been picked up over the years from relatives, from friends, or in company, such as at the *ceilidhs*. Always I have felt myself at a great disadvantage, for the best tales are related in

II

the Gaelic, whose nuances and asides, for which there are no equivalents in the English tongue, eluded me. When I was a boy at school, sadly enough the Gaelic tongue was not only forbidden within the school precincts, but strapped out of us if we were overheard using it by the 'Ragie auld Billie' of a prejudiced headmaster — although to be fair even to him, he was only carrying out the 'educational' policy laid down by distant and culturally blind administrators. My home lay a mile or two from the village, so I never mixed enough with the other youngsters to pick up much of the Gaelic, for most of them were even then bi-lingual, and the English tongue, as ever, proved pervasive.

When writing down these tales — and a great labour of love it has been — I have tried hard to capture the lovely rythms of the island speech. That has not been too difficult, perhaps, for I am told often enough that my own tongue, even after all these years, still carries the distinctive brand of the Islanders' use of English. I have been concerned, though, about trying to write direct speech in the dialect and accent of the island. I was encouraged, though, by re-reading the wonderful Para Handy tales by the late, great, and much lamented Neil Munro — not that I am making any foolish comparison with his genius! But he made his unforgettable characters spring to life partly by the skilful use of dialect. I have tried to do that, too, encouraged by his example.

Again I was always fascinated by the knowledgeable writings about folklore and places in the Highlands and Islands by the late Seton Gordon. In our lengthy exchanges of correspondence he gave me much useful information on Mull people and folklore, which he generously invited me to quote in my own writings.

In this connection, I should like to pay tribute to Alastair Phillips, who, although retired from the staff of the *Glasgow*

Herald, is still an active writer. He started me off in writing as a hobby — quite by accident — when he published an amusing reference to my vintage motor car (known as *'Rosinante'*) which caught his attention one day parked in Buchanan Street outside the 'Herald' offices. I replied to this with an indignant but whimsical tribute to my horseless carriage (a very appropriate description!), which he actually published. Over the years we began to create imaginary characters and exchanged anecdotes in his popular 'Editorial Diary', in which he was once kind enough to describe me as his favourite correspondent. From him I learned something of the art of expression and a few of my stories began to appear in the Weekend Page of the *Glasgow Herald*, including some now used in this collection, such as 'The Ramshorn Crook'. I am grateful to the *Glasgow Herald* for permission to reprint these. I wonder if Alastair Phillips now remembers our exchanges?

Besides the *Glasgow Herald*, I am indebted to the *Scots Magazine*, of Dundee, for publishing my stories from time to time, including such as 'Lawful Occasions' and 'The Two Herdsmen'. Another publication from Thomson's of Dundee, *'The Peoples' Friend'*, published 'The Busy Street' not so long ago. I greatly appreciate their permission to reprint them now, and all their cooperation, together with the good wishes they all expressed for the success of 'Tall Tales'.

My object in bringing together this collection of assorted stories is in its own small way to preserve these old tales which might otherwise be lost and forgotten for ever when the tellers of the tales pass on. Our Highland Heritage is a precious thing which is being slowly and inevitably eroded by the sophistication of modern times. Only by written records can we preserve for future generations something of the way of life of our forefathers.

I have written, broadcast and lectured about Mull —*'Of Isles*

IV

the Fairest' as the old song has it — and I am of the unswerving opinion that nowhere else in the world will you find a better way of life, nor a finer people with whom to share it.

Peter Angus Macnab
Dervaig,
Isle of Mull.

WATER UNDER THE BRIDGE

1

WATER UNDER THE BRIDGE

Today, if you are passing along the main road a mile or so above the town, you will notice a flat, grassy stretch of five acres surrounded by a crumbling drystone wall, within a shining loop of the Highland burn that winds through the valley. A little isolated house and a few garden walls are all that is left now of a great sprawling building of two storeys built in 1862 to accomodate destitute, despairing people dispossessed of their lands and houses as a result of the widespread clearances in the area.

Here, when the building was neat and trim and the people for whom it had been built comfortable and well cared for, before the place had served its purpose and been vacated, becoming in time an ugly ruin that was finally demolished: here lived the boy when all the world was young. Life for him centred in, on, and beside the river, as he called it. For him, like Tay or Tweed, every pool had its private name, and he came to know every stone and eddy along its course, every corner where a trout lay. From the time he could toddle, the thrill of angling was in his blood. Starting with a long switch cut from a willow tree, with a short fixed line, he graduated to a made-up rod, not very long, certainly, spliced in places and cranky at its only joint. However, it sported a small reel that even worked sometimes. Hooks were 'to gut' — no nylon then. At two for one penny their replacement when lost on underwater snags could be a sore drain on his finances, depending as they did on the sale of an occasional empty bottle to the local grocer. But the boy was proud of that rod.

How he loved one of those mornings after heavy rain, with the trailing mists rising quickly from the hilltops before the sun, the level of the river dropping, but still high, the sun glinting on the amber flood.   Later in life he was reminded of those days when he read the lines:-

'.....on the moors today
The hare is running races in her mirth
And with her feet she from the plashy earth
Raises a mist, that, glittering in the sun
Runs with her all the way, wherever she doth run.'

A big plate of porridge and milk is gulped down with eager impatience.   A cup of tea and a fresh girdle scone rich with butter and bramble jelly.   Then down the stairs three at a time to where the river is calling.   One leap behind follows his big beardie collie Barry, skidding wildly on the polished linoleum and barking with frenzied excitement: Barry, who smiled with long pink tongue at the boy's successes, or whined with grave sympathy when things went wrong.

Pick the rod off its pegs in the bicycle house.   Run round the trim path beside the wall to the smithy, where the tools are stored.   Choose a graip — a potato fork will do — then over to the midden where the earth, rich with years of stored natural fertilisers, soon filled the little tin with assorted worms: big fat long ones for an expedition to the distant lochs, medium ones for the river and — somewhat rare — juicy little striped ones with an aroma of decayed cabbages which the trout found irresistible.   Wipe the tines of the graip and replace it in the smithy.   A sheer waste of time, this, but father will be wrathful if dirty tools are left lying about.

Over the little bridge between the willows and the rhododendron, with a peremptory whistle to Barry, who in his exuberance is chasing a straying hen in an explosion of feathers.   Under the bridge itself there is a shallow pool below a shelf of smooth black basalt.   Canny now, the time for hurry is over.   A worm is slipped over the barb and shank of the hook with practised fingers. Just enough line let out for an underhand cast over to the edge of the eddy where the bait is drawn under the patches of foam.

Yes, right away the line checks unnaturally against the current; there is that unmistakable vibration that runs up line, rod and arm, setting the heart of every true angler thumping with anticipation. Lift the point of the rod until the fish is just felt against the shortened line — then a quick heave and a flapping trout is swung out and on to the bank, where Barry wags his tail approvingly. This time, however, the fish is too small to keep, and being lightly hooked is gently freed and released into the edge of the stream. Nothing else doing here. The boy developed an instinct in those early years about when it pays to stay and fish, or to move on, that stayed with him all his life.

Down to the Willows Pool, deep, long and dark, where grubs and caterpillars drop from the gracefully bending branches to the trout waiting below. A gentle cast sends the worm just below the undercut grassy bank golden with marsh marigolds. Let out more line and follow it downstream. Then just at the big overhang, where trailing bog myrtle holds the debris of recent floods, there is a quick check, the tug of a good fish, and the line goes slicing upstream against the current. Tighten up — guess the size — yes, it can just be done — and out swings another trout, a good one this time of six or seven ounces. Tap its head smartly agains the heel of the old, battered, too-big ex-army boots the boy is wearing; admire the gold and silver scales, the red spots, the creamy line edging the ventral fin, then the fish is slipped into the satchel at the boy's side. And so the morning goes on.

With the cranky old rod it is essential to judge the weight of a fish before heaving it out. The river holds an occasional giant trout up to a pound or over in weight, sometimes in the most unexpected places. For instance, there was that experience in the Garden Pool. The boy had dropped the worm just as usual below the

4

fence and followed it with the rod point just skimming the tips of the heather and dog rose bushes under which the current bit deeply into the peaty bank. There came quite an ordinary tug, to which he responded with a normal lift and heave. This was rudely checked in mid-air as a vast fish, a golden beauty, came flapping half out of the water. The sudden check was too much for the rod, which snapped in two places; the frayed hook parted, and the monster vanished in a depth charge of spray. Despondently the boy and his dog crept back home with a massive repair job for father to carry out.

A good lesson for all time, especially for the great days to come when the boy, taller and stronger, finally substituted the fly for the worm after being given the most wonderful present of all time — a fine, brand new greenheart rod, reel and line. After that he forsook the river and haunted the distant lochs with their great, wary sporting trout.

By pools, rocks and gravelly runs the river wound its way downstream for half a mile before losing itself for a while in the deep holes among the peat hags. Along its banks were many diversions. There were banks where the wild strawberries grew in delicious profusion. A rabbit warren, where Barry stalked baby rabbits and brought them to hand unharmed, to be reared at home as pets. The weedy pond beloved by frogs and newts, where the first frogs' eggs of the year were to be found.

The lower point of the boy's 'beat' ended at the 'Big Ling' (Linn), the first of the deep black reaches, useless for the worm but a good training ground for the fly, and a magnificent swimming pool on the hot summer days. Here were yellow and white water lilies, beds of tall reeds and rushes where the mallard ducks reared their broods of brown downy ducklings. There was more variety upstream from the house. There was a tiny woodland tributary where the boy once had the unique experience of watching an adder coiled round a projecting branch bending down gracefully to sip the water, like a bird drinking.   There were many adders along the riverside, timid, and disappearing at his approach, but the few he did see were given a wide berth.

More adventurous were the limitless horizons beyond.   Here lay the Stuc, the waterfall whose wide pool held the mightiest fish in the river over there beneath the hazel trees that leaned far out from the steep bank above.   In late Autumn the boy used to swing far out above the pool on their bending branches reaching for the clusters of big sweet brown hazel nuts, the biggest of which were always just beyond his finger tips.   Oh, it was an exciting pool!   Edging out across a slippery apron of smooth basalt covered by the thin spread of water he could cast just far enough to drop the worm at the near edge of the wide revolving pancake of foam under which the monster fish lay.

Their origin was a mystery.   Some people thought they were sea-trout now dull and spent after fighting their way up the lower cataracts and falls from the sea.   The boy disagreed, never having seen a sea-trout in the river in all his experience.   He submitted they were simply big trout that had come down the overflow at the lochs during a spate.   Anyway, they could not be heaved unceremoniously out of the water; not until they had fought it out, sometimes to the limit of rod and line, and then been dragged precariously across the shelving rock to the grassy bank where they were despatched at 'Execution Rock', the big square rock on which the boy then sat re-living his experience.

Above the Falls Pool the river divided into two branches.   One could be explored past the reservoir, across the moor, to the foot of the bold escarpment of the Crater Hill, from whose summit loch it emerged as an underground stream.   This was the loch whose black, unplumbed depths were feared — until later, when the boy found there were trout there as well, and good ones, too, if darkish in colour.   Up here on the moor were curious grassy circles in the heather marking the sites of ancient dwellings, their walls now level with the ground, each containing in its centre the clumps of nettles that mark where man has been. The boy regarded this as an uncanny place frequented by the Little People, to be passed quickly, with eyes averted.

The other branch of the river wound its way to the west and found its source at the overflow from the lowest of three of the finest fishing lochs man or boy could desire. In the next few years the boy came to know every bay, bank, headland and weed bed, where there lived a stock of trout whose characteristics identified at a glance the exact spot where it had been caught. Of course, admittedly the boy was somewhat distracted at times by having to keep an eye on the skyline for the keeper, or even for the proprietor himself. Now, with almost a lifetime behind him, the boy remembers how with his unsophisticated tackle and less expertise his catches were better than they are now with the best of equipment. Perhaps it is the fish that have changed. Anyway, as he grew older, he became increasingly aware that the greatest satisfaction comes not from the catching of fish, but from perfection in the art of fishing.

Enough for the boy to have as his own the river in all its moods, that looped his home in a silver cord, talking all the summer nights to the quiet woods, and which in return gave him of its secrets. During the summer months when school was an unpleasant memory or a vague future threat, when the water was low, he swam in the pools or sailed his little ships in the shallow reach of the Henhouse Pool behind the house. In his imagination they were transformed into lymphads upon the loch, the galley of Kishmul, dirty British coasters, or sleek swift warships dealing out death and destruction along a hostile coast, or exploring the cataracts and waters of an unknown coast. By a quick turnaround he was in the defending forts bombarding the raiding fleet with shells made of dried peat which burst convincingly. It all depended on what book he was reading at the time.

But the years went on inevitably. The boy became aware that the Great Days were sadly drifting away beyond recall. In front lay the greatest adventure of all, to go away into the wider world far from his island and the beloved river — even though he was to return in years to come. Before the day of his departure came round he performed one symbolic rite, a sacrifice to the spirit of the river. When the very skies were weeping and the river roared sullenly **bank-high**, he launched his cherished boats one by one into the swift current and sadly watched them borne swiftly out of sight towards the distant sea and the realms of adventure into which he himself was to follow.

THE BUSY STREET

THE BUSY STREET

I am sitting here now with the years behind me on the low stone wall in front of the little cottage, a natural seat worn smooth by the posteriors of generations before me.   This is where we sit when the weather is fine, watching the world going by, until — as the poet says —'We tired the sun with talking, and sent him down the sky' with our arguments and discussions and stories of the days of long ago.   In front of us a miniature timber yard of spent matches gathers in a semi-circle, and clouds of tobacco smoke from well-charred pipes keep the clouds of frustrated midges at a respectable distance.

If you are interested, the cottage is one of a pair in a village originally of twenty-six houses, each with its long garden at the back and grazing rights on the hill, built back in 1799 by Maclean of Coll, one of the more enlightened of the old landlords.   Not that he would recognise the place today if he could see it, what with the extensions and face-lifts that have transformed them into modern homes or holiday houses.   The single street runs along a hidden shelf of basalt that nearly bankrupted the contractors when they were laying our fine new water supply a few years ago.

Through the spaces between the houses in front of us we can watch the uneasy tides moving slowly up the narrow sea loch and reluctantly receding, leaving the seaware bright and refreshed where it covers the rocky shore in a slippery mantle, and spreading a feast of sea foods on the dark sands over which the gulls, oyster-catchers and the village ducks and geese honk, squabble and cry noisily.   Out there the salmon and seatrout cruise in and out with the tide, awaiting the rains which will flood the river and allow them to ascend joyfully to the gravelly redds away up the glen, below the green corries where the deer lie hidden in the deep bracken and heather.   When the luminous darkness of a Hebridean night comes down, the deer, always led by a suspicious old hind with twitching ears, come quietly down to graze on the tender crops of the low-lying croft lands.   That is why I keep the old salmon rod handy on top of the shelf and the gun under the mattress.

That is the background of our little village: but indeed it is a busy place and there is always something going on along the street. Early in the morning the Forestry van, with its load of workers, leaves from in front of the Post Office, returning at noon, away again, then home for the day just after five.   Like the Posty's van from the distant car ferry terminus, its movements mark the passing of the hours.

After breakfast the older children trail their feet reluctantly to school, swinging their satchels and exchanging excited small-talk in their fascinating lilting dialects.   In my young days it would have been in the Gaelic, but only the old folk really have it now-a-days.   Soon afterwards the milk comes round in an old estate car, with a cheerful accompaniment of clashing cans, morning news and child noises from a nimbus of tiny children too young to go to school.

Then as regular as clockwork, along comes old Alasdair Susie.   If you ask the folk why he is called that, they will look at you as if you are very far back mentally and say *'Because his mother was a MacNeill, of course!'*   He hirples past on his way to the communal pump (he has not yet had the water installed in his house), balancing his sore hip with two pails instead of his usual home-made stick.   He always has plenty to talk about, so on the way back he joins us for a smoke. His latest grievance is the action of some blaggards that set off no less than three heather fires in the past week; the boldness of them, putting a match at the very edge of the road at that! A good job, we agree, that with the east wind blowing and a month's drought behind it the fires stopped at the very edge of the Allt Uaine burn. Man, if they had jumped it the whole glen would have gone up, plantations and all. Yes, the Forestry was quick on the scene and they are saying the Police have their eye on a certain pair well known to us.

Then Spot comes trotting along the street, talking volubly with his tail and smiling ingratiatingly, looking for his biscuit. I keep an old stale packet for him on the kitchen dresser; and although I know fine he would prefer a nice fresh crisp one, and he toys with the biscuit I offer him, he finally swallows it. No doubt he is thinking in his doggy mind, as he cocks his lugs along the street, that if he refused the biscuit, sure enough his sworn rival Roy, that spoilt collie from the hotel, would come for it and not be so particular. A greedy one, that Roy! He'd better no' show his face at this end of the village!

But just now all we can see in front of the hotel is a distant wisp of hair, two pert ears and a pair of button eyes peering out where Grisach, the tiny Cairn terrier, is lying as usual in the exact middle of the road. She won't budge, no, not even for the Police car with the sergeant himself in it. She might as well be a "Keep Left" sign!

Along the other way I see Spot sidling stiff-legged past Alexa Bean, who is sitting in her front porch surrounded by her retinue of six cats, every one smug and fat, with its front paws neatly folded under its chest. You'd think butter wouldn't melt in their mouths — all but the *Puseag Ruadh* with his tatty ear. He looks out of place in that domestic circle; he would be happier prowling around back gardens, raising merry hell just after people had settled down for the night at one in the morning — for we villagers keep early hours. You would think Alexa Bean would be spending a fortune on cat food, but no fear! They can fight it out round the one wee saucer: but you never saw such a bunch of thieves. Not a kitchen window can be left open, not by the width of a paw.

Ah — here comes Merac the sheep and her two lambs from the direction of the manse. (Poor minister! I'm afraid he has been leaving the garden gate open again!) They are systematically working over the few struggling plots that try to make a show in front of the houses. Merac thrives on rambler roses, so if they don't grow fast enough to outreach her they just vanish. The lambs, too, are appreciative, and learning fast. In a few months' time they will finish off with their agility what their ageing mother has unavoidably spared.

We watch the slow procession of cows swaying lazily along the middle of the street. On their outward journey they are thinking of lush grass and cool waters; coming home, to an accompaniment of gastric rumblings, they are looking forward to the relief of milking and relaxation in the dim, quiet byre, far from the maddening attentions of flies. But oh, the street after they have passed!

Before leaving the subject of animals, I must say how we still miss the old ram who used to stravaig through the village before Merac came on the scene. We called him The Provost because of his long nose and straggling whiskers. Poor old Provost; he became very poorly and died a year ago in a little hollow by the bridge, where he lay for quite a while before his presence became increasingly obvious. However, he had a fine pair of curly horns I managed to salvage on the quiet with a Bushman saw and a towel round my face, and duly turned them into a couple of nice crook handles.

He loved dust bins, did The Provost, which he knocked over in his early morning round, pawing over the contents for tit-bits. There was one terrible fright he gave to the whole village early one dark morning. There came a sudden banging and smashing like a boiler shop that brought people leaping from their beds. Lights came on in all the houses (oh yes, we all have the electrics), doors opened and men came cautiously out stuffing shirt tails into hastily donned trousers and carrying hammers, axes, spades — just whatever came to hand in the hall stand at the front door. I had the gun out myself. But what do you think? The Provost had poked his greedy head into one dust bin too many and become jammed by his curly horns. There he was backing and charging like a tank, and before we could pin him down he had smashed in two garage doors, all the glass that was still left in the telephone box and twenty yards of a newly painted fence.

One passer-by that caused a different kind of alarm last winter was the tall grey horse from Torr-an-Eas. How he got out of the field we never knew, for the old double bed they used for a gate was still in position; but out he got and came looming slowly along the dark street. The Womens' Rural was just coming out of the hall from their whist drive — and my goodness, the screamings and faintings! Just at that Archie the Fish was coming along late in his wee van when he was confronted by this big thing in his dim sidelights (the headlamps never worked). The van finished up on Alexa Bean's front steps and when Archie burst through the door of his house a few seconds later (and, mind you, it is a quarter of a mile away) he gasped out to his wife that ass sure ass he wass standing there.....'In the street before me wass the Pale Horse of the Revalaation and on its back the ghost of Eoghann a'Chinn Bhig with his claymore in one hand and his head underneath the other one.....' Poor Archie didn't touch a drop for at least a week afterwards.

We get great entertainment from some of the summer visitors walking past, but particularly yon long-haired weirdies who live as natural curiosities in a place outside the village like the colony of grey seals over on the west coast. Their displays of bosoms and buttocks may suit the younger folk, but for us it is simply a new subject for discussion, wondering as we do if they are actually wearing garments, or if these are painted on.   I do believe that for the first time in their lives they feel a little uneasy when they pass in front of our silent critical gallery; but if the poor souls could only understand the remarks passed by us afterwards they would be off the island by the next ferry.

As we slowly review the affairs of the island over our last pipe for the day, we smile with amused toleration at some of the summer visitors who think our little village is a quiet backwater in an island where is is nothing to see and little to do.   Man, are they no' far back!

THE MAN FROM GLACGUGAIRIDH

Once upon time Eachann Ban, in Glacgugairidh (which, as everyone knows, lies between Reudle and Haunn), was given a present of the fantastic sum of £100 by his grandfather, who must undoubtedly have been past his best. Anyway, in this spirit of benevolence he said to Eachann, who was his favourite grandson, 'You haf always been good to me and doing aal the chobs, and you haf neffer had a holiday out of Glacgugairidh. Away you go to London and enchoy yourself with the money.' What happened is best described in the words of Eachann himself on his return after his adventures among the bright lights.

'I manached to get fixed up at a hotel and the first night I went out for a walk. Ther wass lots of people about: oh, far more than at Glacgugairidh, and no end to the houses. Now, if I wass at home they would aal be stopping and speaking to me, but in London nobody stopped; so I went back to the hotel. "What queer people you haf in London compared with Glacgugairidh," I said to the manager. "Not a person hass spoke to me from the time I went out."

' "Well now," said the manager, "Tomorrow night late on chust you take a walk along the street near Waterloo Station and you will find plenty that will be speaking to you."

'So the night after, away I went; and right enough, the people began to smile and start to speak: but it wass a strange thing — they wass aal ladies. At last one stopped me; a fine-looking black woman she wass. "I'm from Uganda," she says. "Wher do you come from?" "Oh, I'm from Glacgugairidh," I replies to her, "And I am here for a holiday with the £100 my grandfather gave me." "Well," she says, "Would you like to come home with me?" —which I thought wass very friendly: but — "What," I said to her, "Aal the way to Uganda?" '.

LAWFUL OCCASIONS

LAWFUL OCCASIONS

.   The island people used to have a refreshing toleration of officialdom and in return the Police maintained a commonsense attitude towards little trifles, which although perhaps strictly irregular, were harming nobody.   Since things were livened up in recent years and the prowl car is liable to come round the corner of the road on inappropriate occasions, people have had to become more circumspect.   Why, they are even penalising a motorist for making no more than a small alteration to the date of his driving licence.   In the old days, the possession of any licence at all, in or out of date, was considered the least important item in driving a car.   I knew a man in the village who drove for three years on the same provisional licence; his car had two of its wings held on with twists of fence wire, no silencer and two half bumpers, to the rearmost of which was attached the tattered fragment of the surviving 'L' plate.

At a farm a few miles along the road and up a fierce Forestry road there were two brothers, each of whom owned an aged but serviceable identical BSA motor cycle.   Each machine had a different registration number in front and behind, but one of the numbers was common to both cycles, on the front of one and the rear of the other.   What happened was that one day one of the brothers ran into a motor car at a sharp corner — where, as he said

18

resentfully, he had never seen a car before — and his front forks were a write-off. About the same time the other brother seized up his back hub and ruined the rear assembly. However, one day over at the market on the mainland a few weeks later they came across a BSA of the same model as their own, with its engine wrecked. They picked it up for a few pounds and took it home.

Well, one brother replaced his front forks and the other the back end of his machine by cannibalising their purchase, and everybody was happy. However, it was too much bother to change over the number plates from the wrecked cycle — so hence the multiplicity of numbers. How did they square things with the Law? You just drive up beside the policeman, if you saw him, and had a chat. It was all right as long as he could see just one end at a time.

Then there was the floating flock of sheep. There were two small sheep farms divided by a common march wall. The two farmers arranged to maintain a number of unmarked — and unidentifiable — sheep either on one side of the dyke or on the other. When the Department man came round to count the sheep for the annual subsidy, this floating flock was slipped through the dyke and included in the count of sheep belonging to the other farmer. As the official had to detour for some distance with his car to reach the second farm, there was ample time to drive the flock back to the other side and have it swell the numbers of the other farmer.

However, in our law-conscious community insulated from the Police by twelve miles of hill roads, officialdom is still kept in its true perspective. Merac Ann, at the telephone exchange opposite the police station, can see out of her window which of the roads the prowl car is taking out of the town. If it seems to be making for our village she lifts the 'phone for a wee chat with Kirsty, our postmistress. In no time at all the bar is organised; every unlicenced gun vanishes, as do the poachers from the banks of the Allt Uaine; wireless sets are out of sight under the beds and unlicenced motor cars invisible under bales of hay.   Why, even all the sheep on the hill have been dipped, and a model community awaits the arrival of the Police.

Not so long ago I had a personal experience of how strictly the local people observe the licencing laws.   Alick Ban and I came up from the lobsters one afternoon and decided to wait for the arrival of the van carrying our friends back from the sales with all the latest news.   Waiting can be thirsty work, especially with the doors of the inn beckoning from just across the road, so I agreed with alacrity when Alick suggested having a glass or two to pass the time.   Brushing aside my timid suggestion that it would not be opening time for another hour or more, he led the way with easy familiarity through the kitchen, smacked the stout cook on her inviting anatomy (and received in return a voluble tirade in forceful Gaelic), and crossed over to the door leading to the bar premises. It was locked, of course, but for greater convenience the key was always hung on a nail beside the door.   Inside, Alick fumbled for a minute with a hand that dwarfed the array of bottles.   'Where iss Lachie keeping the key now?' he complained.   'See if you can find it.'

We lifted the key from the angle of the counter, and with a speculative glance over the bottles, brass handles and under-the-counter paraphernalia, we unlocked the bar door and stepped into the public area in front of the counter, where Alick rang the service bell.   Presently Lachie came in from the garden, rubbing his hands on an old potato sack, and set up a couple of small sensations for us, drawing a half pint for himself: so we settled down for a smoke and a crack.   We were joined presently by Archie the Fish, Pate, and the old retired school-master.

Soon afterwards the arrival of the expected van shattered the peace outside with a pig-like squealing of brakes, erupting an incredible crowd of sheep farmers, shepherds, and their dogs, all excited and voluble after a succesful day at the sales.   They, too, came swarming through the kitchen, crowding Lachie against the bar handles as they pushed past in a tangle of tweeds, sheep smells and yelping dogs unavoidably trodden upon in the crush.

A head above them all was big MacIan, from Minganish, away up the glen, whom they called Iron Hut MacIan because his grandfather was the first man in the island to put up corrugated iron shelters for the sheep at lambing time. His lambs had topped last year's prices by no less than ten shillings, which called for a celebration: so into every man's hand he thrust a glass just as fast as Lachie could fill it. I happened to be standing at the end of the counter, just near enough to overhear a confidential business talk between Lachie and himself, which revealed how simply and sensibly the liquor trade is conducted in our happy village.

'Lachie,' said MacIan in a penetrating whisper and leaning over the counter, 'Am I no' owing you something for a while now?' The proprietor pulled out a black-covered exercise book boldly printed 'Property of Argyll County Council Education Authority' from the back of a drawer and began to run a finger down its lengthy columns of entries.

'Ther wass twelve cans of beer and the bottle I gave the boy the day before the dipping,' he began, jotting down the amount on the back of an old label: 'Then the night after that there wass the six men came in for haffs — you told them to tell me it would be aal right.' Then a page or two later — 'Ther wass the ten pounds you got from me the day you missed the bank van — oh yess, and here's a bottle the day of the games.'

'Do you no' mean the day of the Show?' queried MacIan.

'Hach, you had two haff bottles that day ass well — do you no' mind?' — 'Yess, yess, that will be right enough. What else?'

A few more items were agreed, jotted down, and finally totalled. 'That will be £27. 5. 8d.' announced Lachie. MacIan, who had pulled out a crumpled cheque book, scrawled his name on a blank form, snicked it out and passed it over. 'Here, Lachie; chust fill it out yourself,' he remarked genially, with a glance at the clock. 'Dhia, iss that the time? Come on, boys, we'll haff to be going.'

With that he tossed of what was left in his glass, gave us greetings all round, and with his companions went out with the stride of a hillman — this time by the front door, which someone had opened earlier, more as a gesture to the clock than as a necessity. We heard the van being persuaded to start, the doors slammed as the passengers piled in; then in a choking cloud of blue smoke, to the accompaniment of clashings and shearings from the transmission and the bellow of a broken silencer, almost drowned by the hysterical barking of the four collie dogs in the back, the equipage faded into the distance.

I turned back to where Alick was holding forth on the subject of the making of hazel crooks, on which he was an admitted authority. 'Three fingers, there should be, between the inside turn of the crook and the shaft,' he averred, demonstrating the measurement on his own stick with three fingers that freely covered the width of my whole hand. 'And be sure the handle iss well fixed to the shaft. I mind the first time Seumas Ban tried to fix on a handle, it pulled off on an old ewe next day when he wass on the hill, and she wass wearing it round her neck like a tiara for a month afterwards.'

'Talking about the Seumas Ruadh,' broke in another of the crowd, 'Do you mind the story they used to tell about Calum MacDougall, the time they wass on the cliffs catching young seumas ruadh for the winter?' (This is the local name for the puffin — *Red Jimmy* — esteemed at one time for its edible properties for which the young were killed and salted down in barrels for the winter.) 'Now Calum had forgotten to bring a piece of rope with him, but he wass wearing a long red scarf that he used to tie together a bunch of the birds by the necks to lower down to the men below the rock. Chust in the middle of it, one of the birds came alive again and gave one jump that whipped the end of the scarf out of Calum's grip. The others fell out, but this one went away with the scarf trailing behind it. Do you know, when they wass out at the lobsters next week, ther wass the Seumas Ruadh sitting on the Sgeir Mhor still wearing Calum's fine red scarf round its neck!'

The laughter that followed was suddenly shattered by a howl of anguish from Lachie behind the bar. 'Tam it all, ther's MacIan away and I forgot to charge him for that round chust now.' He hurled his exercise book back into the drawer. 'My chove,' he added gloomily, 'I'll haf the duvvle of a chob to explain that to him when we sort it out again in the Spring!'

BOAT OF MANY COLOURS

Ian Gearr — that is, Short, or Dumpy John — was a MacIan of Ardnamurchan who lived over in Mingary Castle, the stronghold of his clan on that wild promontory. He was an inveterate raider of the eighteenth century, notorious for his cattle lifting and near-piracy. In fact, he was so well known in this respect that he resorted to all kinds of tricks to avoid detection.

For instance, he was reputed never to paint both sides of his galley the same colour, and often re-painted it, as well as changing the colour of his sail. Thus, when he was reported from one place as having been on one of his expeditions with a green boat, he was defended by people elsewhere, who, seeing the boat from a different angle, swore it was black and not green, and couldn't be the same boat!

OUT FOR A DUCK

OUT FOR A DUCK

Hughie and I were passing Betsy's cottage (that is, Betsy Donnacha, not to be confused with Betsy Challum, who lives in the Council Houses above the village), just as she came stumping out, dragging yon black hat of hers down to her ears, and leaving the front door on the sneck.   Even today few people lock their doors in the village.   Partly to herself, partly to benefit our casual ears, she shouted (for she was very deaf) — 'I'll away down to the shop, for I haven't a scrap of butter in the house.   The duck will do fine till I get back.'

Now, Hughie and I were young then, with appetites sharpened by days on the hill, clean salt winds, and now by a whiff of savoury cooking coming out the door.   We looked at each other, then down the road, which was deserted except for Betsy, who was just disappearing round the bend at the bridge, and two of Lachie's cows grazing their way homewards along the verges of the road.   It would do no harm to have a look, we agreed.   So we lifted the loop of string that held the front gate.   As we opened the front door the aroma of cooking duck became irresistible, and we moved into the kitchen.   There, indeed, a fat duck was gently simmering in a big pot over a low calor gas flame, swimming in rich, fat gravy soup with barley and all the rest that set our teeth watering.

26

'Betsy won't be back for ages,' remarked Hughie: 'I don't think she'd ever notice if we tried a slice or two and a spoonful of soup.' So we took two plates from the dresser and knives and spoons from the drawer. I don't know how Betsy would have set about carving the duck, but we didn't waste time looking for the carver. Hughie pulled out his razor-sharp claspknife, wiped the blade carefully on his sleeve (for he was always hygienic where food was concerned, was Hughie), gripped one of the legs and turned the duck over. I ladled two small helpings of soup into a couple of plates.

However, like the taste of liquor to an alcoholic, or a reefer to a drug addict (or so we had been told), this proved to be no more than an appetiser. Fifteen minutes later there was still no sign of Betsy, who had become involved with a group of friends outside the Post Office. There was no sign of the duck, either, for it had been converted into a clean pile of bones and drumsticks. Our plates, steadily replenished, had disposed of the soup and only a film of grease remained in the pot.

Hughie sat back with gusty appreciation, wiped his greasy mouth and announced — 'My chove, but that wass good!' But with a sudden note of alarm he added — 'But what are we going to say to Betsy?'

We thought over this for what seemed a long time, with quick glances through the front window to see if the formidable Betsy was coming, for she had a tongue and a memory.

'Hughie,' I remarked at length, 'You know how absent minded she is. Now suppose we just try to clean everything up and put it away.....you know.....as if it had never been.....maybe she will forget.....?'

So we got busy, with time running out. A kettle of water was simmering on the stove, so we hastily boiled it over the gas and every knife, fork and spoon cleaned, dried and put away exactly where we had found it. The pan was scoured and put up on the top shelf with its neighbours. The bones and scraps were dug deep into the potato patch in the back garden. Oh, it was beautifully timed, for we were just halfway along to the bridge when we met Betsy returning and having a loud conversation with herself.

We overheard the sequel next day as we were standing near the butcher's van waiting our turn. Betsy's voice was booming away inside — perhaps there was for once a note of uncertainty in it — '.....could have sworn I had a duck in the house to last me over the weekend.....but there, I'm getting that absent minded. Give me half a pound of mince and see that it's fresher than last time.....'

A CHAPTER FOR ANGLERS

A CHAPTER FOR ANGLERS

Yes indeed, times have changed since the old days when I had those fine lochs almost to myself. Conveniently close to the road, they have turned into a free-for-all. They are fished by newcomers and visitors, most of whom, poor souls, have never known anything better than the mechanical spinning-rod — The Mangle, as we call it in enlightened circles: or most revolting of all, the bubble float, with several tangles of worms impaled on sets of murderous hooks suspended in the water. Good enough for children, to arouse and develop the true angling instincts, but for grown-ups.....Those so-called anglers might as well be sitting in a camp chair with their rod propped over a canal bank for all the fun they get out of fishing. The poor trout are hard put to it to weave their way through the submarine menaces without accidentally hooking themselves. But worse than that, one evening I saw two men working the 'Otter' quite brazenly on the opposite side of the loch. You know the contraption, a weighted board floating edge up that can be angled out into the middle of the loch by pulling on a long string — the principle of the kite. It trails behind it dozens of flies and can be lethal when the fish are rising freely. Unfortunately the operations were being conducted on the other side of the loch, or there might have been some fun.

Now, you won't all agree with my purist principles; so let me branch out and tell you about one particular outing that sticks in my memory from the old days; actually two incidents diametrically opposite in their outcome. I remember the light breeze blowing from the south-west, the summer sky dappled with cirro-cumulus clouds like flocks of cloud-sheep, the filtered sunshine that seemed to make our flies move more convincingly in the water. When you learn that I had the privilege of the estate boat for the day and at the oars was the incomparable Do'l Gorm, you will appreciate why I echoed the words of the poet — *'How rich and great the times now are!*

Before I go any further, I must tell you about Do'l Gorm, one of my greatest friends. A roadman of the old school, a craftsman in his trade and something of a practical geologist, wise in the ways of wildlife, a crack shot and deft with the oars. He was mild and inoffensive, a great raconteur and not unacquainted with the way of a stag on the hill and a salmon in the pool. However, he was choosy in his favours; you had to be *en rapport* — *simpatico* — before he would handle a boat for you, and neither rank nor money could entice him. He had a nose for the fish. I've seen us casting away with little success; suddenly he would stir uneasily, cock an eye to the middle distance and say: 'Do you no' think we should maybe be trying the green bank?' Or it might be the reed bed, the old wall, the island drift — and sure enough his hunch would lead us to rising fish.

This particular day he, too was at peace with the world, humming a Gaelic air deep among his whiskers. His foreman was away with a gang clearing a rockfall on the Gribun road, and the surveyor was on holiday. Besides, his piecework in the quarry above the lochs was well up to date, so there he was sitting in the bow seat dropping his flies along his arc of the half circle in front of the boat. We had almost reached the end of the drift that takes you past the steep rocky bank with its fringe of tall bracken and coarse heather and the screen of birch and hazel behind which, as a boy, I used to sit in impatient concealment while the laird and his ghillie rowed past on their way to the other lochs. Not that the laird would have minded much if he had seen me casting away there off the bank — but after all, it was his loch and in deference to his presence I kept out of sight.

We drifted past the lichened old birch tree that leans far out over the water, its roots providing a deep holt for generations of otters, its top branches preserving memories of hung-up casts and lost flies when fishing off the bank. Just beyond it there is a wide, deep inlet ending in an immense field of creamy white water lilies that spread from a basket-full sunk in a corner fifty years before, backed by a stand of tall thick rushes, and behind that the steep slope of the hill with its rocks, heather and bushes faithfully reflected in the still water.

As we drifted bows-out from under the trees I was casting inshore from the stern towards the water lilies. It was dead calm in there, so Do'l Gorm set down his rod and began to edge the boat towards the steady offshore ripple. I noticed the dimpled rings of a few rising trout and was just about to remark that the afternoon rise was about due when something like a depth charge went off in the calm water in front of me, shattering the reflections. The rod point dipped and the line shot out between my slack fingers. I was into a big fish. No artistic timing, tightening, striking — just a smash and grab by a big fish now whipping the line off the screaming reel as it shot away towards the sanctuary of the tangled roots of the lily bed thirty yards away. I had to be brutal, or fish and flies would be gone.

The rod doubled fantastically and the line vibrated. I can tell you I was trembling with excitement as the fish fought with every wile it knew to reach safety. But suddenly it changed its mind, turned and shot back towards the boat. Real danger if it went underneath, and I desperately retrieved the slack line by hand. My companion expertly slid the stern away as the line cut past within inches. When I restored the tension, the fish gave one huge leap, I'm sure a yard out of the water, a big golden trout, but I managed to ease off in time.

Do'l Gorm brought the boat round upwind of the fish, for now we were safely out in the gentle ripple of the open water. Now it was just a matter of time, although some of the rushes made by the fish tore yards of line off the reel, and once it bored in a complete circle right round the boat. As it began to tire, Do'l Gorm drew in the oars and reached for the landing net. At last I eased the fish close enough on a shortened line, the ring of the net went under and up, and the lovely fish was in the boat.

When I think of the beauty of that fish I have a small pang of regret at bringing about its untimely end. I almost believe that if I caught another such trout now-a-days when fishing on my own I should admire it, verify its vital statistics quickly for the record, and slip it back into the water to fight another day! It was a unique fish for our lochs, unusually stumpy for its eighteen inches, with a small head, and weighing over three pounds. In all my years of fishing there I caught only one that remotely resembled it; a fish taken in a few inches of water on a lee shore where it was gulping down flies, snatching one of mine as I dropped it in casually in the passing.

Well, we took a few more nice fish that day and on many days after that, but I never forgot that perfect combination of weather conditions, fish, and companionship.

Mind you, a perfect fishing day is highly unusual. As Do'l Gorm said: 'If the fish iss not thrawn to take, it iss the wind or the weather; too hot or too cold; too many white clouds or clear skies; or else the tackle, or the wrong flies. Or else the fish iss not moving; and when they do start, the keeper comes round the corner of the road and you haf to pack up fast and clear out. For instance,' he continued, 'There wass the day Lachie and me went to fish Loch Frisa.' (Lachie was his boon companion.)

He described how they had the use of the boat kept on the loch by one of the local hotels where at the time there were no fishing guests.   It was a long walk from the town, five miles by the pony track across the shoulder of the Big Hill; but once on the loch the two of them would be as good as the gentry with their sandwiches, a big bottle of *uisge beatha* and their consoling pipes to smoke.

Do'l Gorm paused reflectively, dragged heavily with drain-pipe noises at his battered briar, removed it for closer inspection, and began an involved process of decarbonising.

'It wass a fine day when we started off,' he continued, 'But a thin cloud wass coming over by the time we reached the wee burn above the loch where we used to sample the top layer of the bottle while Lachie steeped his sore feet in a wee pool.   Oh, it wass a special bottle, I mind, with more stars on the label than what I wass seeing the dark night I walked into the signpost at the crossroads.   Lachie wass chust pulling it out of that old bag of his to pass it over to me when it caught, slipped through his fingers and went SMASH! on the stones.   Every drop went down the burn.   Man, man, wassn't that a terrible start to the day?   It wass like an omen.'

Depressed afresh by the memory, he went on to describe how the sky became overcast and by the time they arrived at the lochside and bailed out the boat (for it was badly kept and leaking), a strong wind was blowing up the loch with an increasing drizzle of rain.   They put up the rods and set off, thinking that even if they did have a hard pull down the loch in the teeth of the wind, at least it would blow them home with the chance of some fish.

Setting the rods in the stern they let out plenty of line, hoping to catch something on the troll, took an oar each and began to pull.   The waves began to rise, and they had to fight to keep the boat a steady fifty yards from the shore along the fishing bank, as we called it, of this long narrow and deep loch.   But not a fish was to be had; and every wee while they had to steady the boat and bail out the water.

Then, as Do'l Gorm described it, 'We wass getting gey tired of it all by the time we reached the sandy bay where we always stopped before turning for home.   Chust ass we landed, the rain began to lash down in buckets and the wind fell away to nothing.   At that very moment the trout began to chump like mad, yess, out of the water under the points of our rods.   We pushed off again and began casting away, but not a fish would touch our flies.   They were chumping the way that makes them fall back on their tails — oh, a bad sign, as you know well yourself.'

So they reeled in, thoroughly disgusted, dragged the boat up on the sand and cowered down in the shelter of a few rocks where they gnawed morosely at their wersh sandwiches.   Poor stuff without a drop to wash them down.

'But neffer mind, Lachie,' remarked Do'l Gorm, 'Pass the matches and we'll haff a smock anyway.'   'You've got them yourself,' returned Lachie.   'I put them down on the thwart beside you in the boat.'   Do'l Gorm hurried over to the boat — but no matches.   Not until he lifted the loose bottom boards and saw their only box disintegrating in three inches of water.

'I can tell you,' continued my friend gloomily, 'It wass with heavy hearts and light stomachs we pushed off on our way home.   And here wass the next of it: out on the loch everything wass changed.   The ferry elements wass against us, for the wind had got up again and veered into the north-west, blowing a gale with solid rain in it that soaked us to the skin in a minute — not that we noticed, for we wass too busy peching at the oars with the spray off the big waves coming over our backs, gaining a yard or two at a time, and then getting blown back when we stopped to bail the tam boat.   No chance of putting out the rods for a troll; they wass safely out of the road in the bows.

'And then — as true ass I am sitting here — when we did get back to the shelter of Boat Bay at the head of the loch (and I don't know yet how we did it) the wind fell away to a light breeze, the clouds cleared away like a curtain and the sun came out in the west. And aal of a sudden the trout began to rise, boiling round us with that *"gloop"* they make when they mean business. We chust sat and looked at each other, and after a while Lachie came out with words in the Gaelic you would be be better off not understanding that rumbled like rocks coming down the Gribun cliffs. "Ach, well," he said when he got his breath back, "We might ass well finish the day with a bag of trout to take home." And right enough, in no time at all we had two dozen of yon fine red Loch Frisa trout in the bag.

'It wass getting dark and not a breath of wind when we pulled the boat up for the day. Neffer haf I seen such mudges, and us without even a pipe to keep them off. Ass you know, I like this mild kind of tobacco myself (Do'l Gorm was always a master of understatement!) but Lachie smocked yon stuff like wet tarry rope that kept the mudges six feet away, but man! they got their own back that night! We packed up and started for home in the half dark, Lachie carrying the fine bag of trout.

'His wife wass still up with the lamp on in the kitchen, and put on the kettle when she heard us at the gate. "My, my, chust look at you!" she cried when she saw us with the water still dripping from us and our faces aal puffed up with the mudges. "Are you not the two great fools!"

' "Tach, we're fine now after the walk," returned Lachie, putting his rod away in the corner. "And we're no' that daft. Chust look you at this fine bag of trout." '

Do'l Gorm sadly described the finale to this day of misfortunes. Lachie hitched round the bag with what seemed surprising ease, considering how stiff his shoulder should have been with carrying two dozen good trout for five miles. As he did so, there was a flop at his feet and when he looked down there was this nice half-pound trout lying at his feet. His face red with mortification, he tore the bag open and turned it upside down. There was nothing in it at all. Nothing. Just a few scales and a smell of fish, and the hole in the corner through which the trout had dropped, one by one, along the track from Loch Frisa to the town.

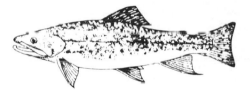

THE SEA POOL

THE SEA POOL

A fortnight had elapsed since the acrimonious exchanges in the bar of the Maclean Arms between Jimmy the Keeper and my old friends Do'l Gorm and his crony Lachie. Jimmy, a huge, red-faced well-nourished Islesman, weighing eighteen stones (even without his boots), was regarded in our community with even more disfavour than the average gamekeeper. Mean, he was, both in his reluctance to stand his hand and in his extra rough treatment of harmless poachers unlucky enough to fall into his big hands. Like a cat, too, on his feet, for all his size.

Anyway, starting with drinks spilt after Jimmy had tripped over Lachie's outstretched feet — quite accidentally, of course — the exchange of recriminations reached a point when the keeper, bursting with rage, bawled at Lachie: '.....you tirty little twister, if I find you ass much ass looking over a bridge at the fush, I'll haf you before the Sheriff — what's left of you!' And when Do'l Gorm tried some mild intervention, Jimmy turned on him snarling — 'Ass for you, you sly old rascal, are you thinking I don't know your ploys over at the Sea Pool? I'm warning you chust this wance —Keep Off! Sir Chon and maself has taken some precaations that will haf you in Court chust like THAT pefore your feet can touch the ground!'

But Do'l Gorm, the imperturbable, gurgling heavily on his pipe and directing a puff of foul-smelling, lung-raxing smoke at the keeper, denied the allegations. 'Man, Chimmy,' he replied virtuously, 'It will be those duvvils over at Portmore you should be talking to. There's nobody here at Calamore would hurt a scale of Sir Chon's salmon.'

Jimmy the Keeper summarised the position in a fine flow of rude words in the Gaelic and boasted rashly to the whole room as he backed out.....'And if any man can get away with a fush from the Sea Pool after this.....I'll.....I'll give him a free permit for the whole river!'

As I said at the start, a fortnight had passed since the keeper threw down the challenge. In response to a hint from Do'l Gorm I was sitting with Lachie and himself on the bales of hay in the loft above the byre.

'There iss a high tide coming,' announced Do'l Gorm, 'And there iss plenty of fush about. Man, it would be a temptation for anybody with a bit of a net and time on his hands to haf a look at the Sea Pool some night. Of coorse, Chimmy and the watchers will be on the look-out. There would haf to be three people to do the chob: one with the boat — maybe that could be me; then Lachie, here, could work the net rope on the shore and keep an eye open for signals from the third man.' He tailed off with a quick side look at me, and suggested diffidently, 'Maybe that could be you?' — adding hastily 'Of coorse, it you wassn't doing anything else that night, and felt like it.' An expression of confidence in my abilities that made me feel very proud. When I nodded, he added 'You could be beside the tree on the top of yon wee cnoc where you could watch and listen both ways. If you will take your wee torch Lachie will be watching for a flash if you are hearing anything. The boat? Ach, she'll be aal right, out near the point with us inshore of her.'

'But what if Jimmy and company come in from the sea?' I

enquired. 'Not him. He iss a landsman; but he will haf plenty of watchers with him. If he sees us he will haf the Police waiting on us when we get back: even in Calamore the telephone iss quicker than we can row.'

Then I had an idea. 'Did you ever hear the story of the galley of MacIan?' I asked. 'Well,' squeaked Lachie uneasily, pulling out his watch, 'Iss it no' getting a bit late.....?' 'Wait, wait,' I added. 'When MacIan was going on one of his raids he would paint his boat white on one side and black on the other, and people ashore never knew whether he was coming or going!'

'My chove, that's a new one,' remarked Do'l Gorm thoughtfully. 'Lachie, you see that we haf that roll of old white sailcloth in the boat and some more rope.'

So in due course we went down the back lane to where our boat was drawn up, with me walking in front to make sure the coast was clear, the others following with two potato sacks containing our gear and a third that gave off a muffled rattle that set Lachie cursing gently when he missed a step. We pushed off and rowed quietly into the still reflections and anonymity of the summer twilight. When we were well out we put our backs into it and in half an hour we were drifting gently to rest off the gravel banks at the mouth of the river that becomes a long deep sea pool when the tide is full in. We eased down the anchor, waited and listened.....listened. Nothing broke the silence but the drowsy murmur of the rapids up the river behind the tree, and the occasional cry of a night bird, and once, high up, the lonely quacking of a belated merganser on its homeward flight. Presently there was a splash, then another as the fish came edging in with the tide, eager and excited at the first touch of fresh water.

We lifted the anchor, moved in past the point and grounded on the shore within the pool. I landed, scouted around for a while then slipped back to report all clear. As I went up to my watching post Lachie came with me on some strange operation involving the third sack, which I now saw contained a dozen or more empty rusted fruit tins, each with one or two small pebbles inside.   Those he set up across the neck of land and connected them all with stretches of old nylon gut about knee high.

'The tins iss far enough away to give you good notice if anybody is coming.' whispered Lachie.   'When they knock one over you will hear it but the watchers will think they are chust tin cans left lying about by the picnickers.   I'll away and help Do'l Gorm — mind the flash on the torch if you hear anything.'

Lachie vanished like a ghost.   Presently the two of them were splashing about making noises that sounded to me like D-Day in the silence, as Do'l Gorm rowed across the pool and the path of the fish with one end of the net, then circled round and back to meet the other end where Lachie on the shore was pulling in the slack like mad after throwing some stones into the water higher up to scare the fish down into the net.

Our general had timed the operation for Jimmy the Keeper's late suppertime, for he was not a man to miss his food.   More splashings.   Muttered exclamations.   A few muffled thuds — good, that meant the net was in and a few fish being despatched. A wee silence fell; in the middle of it I heard the first rattle of a tin — then another — and faintly I heard the keeper snarling in an undertone — 'Eesht!   Mind your ploddy feet!'   With an occasional quick flash from my hooded torch I flitted down to the boat.   Pack up,' I whispered.   'They're at the tree by now.'

Already the fish were in a sack, the net into another and both slung into the boat.   As Lachie and I stepped in and Do'l Gorm in the bows pushed off, a howl arose behind us like a pack of hounds as the watchers heard us and saw the dim figures at the boat.   'Keep you down,' our leader muttered to me, and as I dropped to the bottom of the boat my two companions bent to the oars and we shot away.   The watchers were on the shore before we had gone forty yards, but all they could see was the outline of two figures tugging at the oars of a white boat — for the bold lads had spread the white sailcloth along the starboard side while we were waiting — and heading south for Portmore.   We could hear big Jimmy bawling with rage, and a battery of guns flashed and banged at us spitefully and quite illegally.   We were well out of range, but it was a good job they weren't rifles.

When we were well out and impossible to be spotted we turned right round and headed north for home, stuffing the white canvas into the sack with the net.   A good job, too, for far behind us a spotlight came on and a speedboat from the slipway below the big house went roaring away out searching for the white boat from Portmore, but it soon faded away into the distance.

We made a detour out to the Sgeir Dubh, an ice-worn tidal reef where at certain times great shoals of lythe and mackerel are to be found above the dense beds of tangle swaying down below in the currents.   Setting up the rods in the stern we trolled for a while and picked up a couple of dozen fish which gave a legitimate atmosphere of fishing, and accounted for the fresh fish scales.   As we came close in to the wooded point at the mouth of the bay we weighted the sack with a few stones from the ballast and put it over the side, attached by a fishing line to a marker in the form of a rusty old tin can.   Backing into the big rocks at the edge of the water I landed and hid the bulky sack with the salmon in a deep hole in the stones above high water mark.

We came boldly into the slipway beside the pier, talking naturally and with our pipes glowing in the darkness; but I had the biggest fright of the night when the floodlight was suddenly switched on above and we saw the two policemen coming down the steps.   What had we done wrong?   However, Do'l Gorm was calmly bending down dividing the fish and putting them on a string for easier carrying as the fat sergeant (we called him The Puffer) put his foot on the gunwale.

'Been at the fushing?' he enquired conversationally.   'Ach, chust one or two for the weekend from the Sgeir Dubh', replied our chief, very civil. 'And did you see anything of a white boat with two men in it?' continued the Puffer. 'Not us,' we averred: 'There wasn't another boat we could see anywhere near the Sgeir Dubh. It would be one of the boats from Portmore you are looking for.'

The constable, a young, keen fellow with an eye on the promotion breadline, stepped into the boat. 'You've no' got many fush there if it was the Sgeir Dubh you were at,' he commmented. 'Chust what we wass saying ourselfs,' agreed Do'l Gorm smoothly, 'And such a fine night for it too.'

But that seemed to be the end of the matter as far as the Police were concerned. Later, when we were quite sure of the movements of Police and public alike, Lachie and I took a walk along the path above the shore and collected the bag of salmon. Six very nice fish.

But wait you: that's not the end of it. When the Post Office van called the day after at Jimmy the Keeper's house (with Calum Post in the know) a parcel, wrapped, stamped, addressed and all was delivered. Inside was a fine ten-pound salmon accompanied by a note in block letters — 'A present from the Sea Pool. Just leave the permit with Big Duncan.'

There must have been a spark of sportsmanship deeply embedded in Jimmy the Keeper's eighteen stones, for right enough, an open permit to fish the river was handed in to Big Duncan at the bar in an envelope addressed simply to *'Do'l Gorm and his friends.'* Not that anybody would ever use it — there's no fun in having a permit to fish. But curiously enough, from that very day we sensed a kind of truce between Jimmy the Keeper and my two friends; and believe it or not, wherever else they operated, not once did they return to the Sea Pool.

EACHANN'S BULL

THE TALE OF EACHANN'S BULL

Every time I see a herd of Highland cattle being driven to the car ferry along the narrow, twisting island roads I think of Eachann and his bull.   Of course, now-a-days we more often see MacBrayne's big cattle float taking over the transportation so much more speedily — and expensively; but there is no romance about that. We cannot see the herdsmen, kenspeckle figures in their day with their navy blue suits, fine black boots, hazel sticks and raincoats slung over their shoulders on a piece of stack rope, with their anxious collie dogs ranging up and down the flanks of their charges.   To some of the herdsmen this was perhaps their annual spree across to the mainland, and coming from the remotest corners of the island, they bore expressions of startled suspicion if addressed by a stranger.   One of them used to be so smartly turned out he was called 'The Duke'.

But Eachann (they called him *Eachann a'gobhar* — Hector the Goat, for some unknown reason) was just another member of of our community whose croft lay up at the Achafraoch.   He is memorable because of his bull.   Now this bull is not to be confused with the famous bull in the Ross of Mull, a quiet Highland beast with horns that spread so wide they could not get it through the door of the byre for the winter.   Not to be outdone, its owner tethered it in the yard and thatched it over against the weather.   Or so the story goes. No, this bull of Eachann's was a real terror of a beast to outsiders, although in the presence of Eachann it was as quiet as a kitten. Why, it loved that man so much it would follow him about mooing lke a calf after a pail of milk. Mind you, it was not much of a bull for looks; on the contrary, it had a back with a bend in it like a line of washing, knob knees and a neck like a sheep's: but for all that he was as proud of that bull as an Argentinian buyer would be of a pedigree beast at the Perth sales.

You see, the bull owed his popularity to the calves that came off him; as ugly as their father — you could tell them on the hill a mile away — but the heifers turned out to be the finest milkers in the island.

Every year when the big Show came round Eachann was urged by his friends to enter the bull for the judging. But no, he said, he was far too nervous to go into the ring with the animal before all the toffs and the judges from the mainland. Mind you, he added, he would have no fears for the bull. The judges could not fail to be impressed by the quality. But wait you: this time his friends got round him one night in the bar of the Maclean Arms when Eachann was full of Dutch courage and persuaded him to enter the bull for the coming show. His pride in the beast blinded him to the fact that they were just having him on, to create the laugh of the year for the critical judges who would be coming from all over Scotland, yes, as far as Fort William.

So the big day came round. Animals came into the show-ground from all over the island: big shaggy Highland cattle, Ayrshire and Friesian milkers, cows with calf at foot, blackfaced sheep from the hills and Cheviots from the home fields, cross lambs, hens and ducks. Even a section for dog trials and pony racing. Of course there was the big marquee for the W.R.I. and home industries where the ladies could fight it out. There was the refreshment tent too, that had to put out a contract for bringing the crates of beer from the pier. Hundreds of class prizes and fifteen pounds and a silver cup for the champion beast of the year. All the gentry were there up for the shootings and fishings, a record crowd of summer visitors, and all the locals. For once the sun was shining, the animals looked their best, never was there such a grand Show.

The morning went on, and at length it was Eachann's turn to lead the bull into the ring in front of the judges. He had been waiting nervously, the bull at his side without even a halter. So into the ring he went with the bull walking close behind him. It was then that I felt really sorry for Eachann. There was his beloved bull ambling round, its back like a washing line, head hanging down, its knees bending; no interest except for its master walking proudly there in front. However, Eachann suddenly became aware of the titters and amused looks as he went past, and he heard some of the remarks of the judges who were making fun of the bull and laughing behind their hands. Now Eachann would not have minded so much if they had been directed at himself — but to make fun of the poor bull! But never mind — although he was deeply insulted, he was all there, and showed no sign of it. He started one more circuit of the ring and when he reached the far end he slipped smartly under the ropes, into the crowd, and disappeared.

The bull kept on, until just opposite the judges it raised it head and saw for the first time that Eachann was no longer there. It became rather nervous, with all the crowd, the noise and the laughing, so it lifted its nose in the air and gave a roar for Eachann to come back. By this time he was three deep in the crowd at the bar in the refreshment tent at the other end of the field.

The laughing stopped like a tap turned off and the judges stotted back. The bull stamped a hoof impatiently and dug a horn in the turf, tearing up a yard or two like those Andalusian bulls in Spain you read about. The judges began to move away, pretending they weren't hurrying, and the crowd began to run.

Then the bull got angry. First of all it tore up some stobs, ropes and all, and the ring came down.   Trailing the tangle behind, it put up its tail and made a rush at the nearest tent.   It happened to be the W.R.I. tent, and when he came through the wall at the other end, horns all hanging with all kinds of women's things, the screamings and hysterics were beyond description.   By the time it had smashed in half the pens and stampeded the beasts, things were looking a little unsettled.   People and animals were running for the hills and jumping across the river.   I saw one of the keepers jumping across a pool he couldn't have cast across with his eighteen-foot greenheart rod.   Hens and ducks were squawking and making for the tree tops.   But it was when the young stirks knocked over the two demonstration beehives that the crisis really came.

The Committee was near demented.   The few of them that could get together called for Eachann to come and catch his bull.   They sent messengers along the road as far as the two hotel bars to look for him, but not a sign of Eachann.   And no wonder, for all the time he was sitting enjoying a few glasses in a quiet corner of the refreshment tent, talking about general subjects with a few acquaintances.   You see, the tent was by now the only one left standing, because it was discreetly sited round the corner behind the trees where the womenfolk couldn't see their men slipping in and out for a refreshment.   At last Eachann was located by the Committee, who accompanied by the judges, came rushing into the tent shouting and waving their fists.

'Away you go at once,' they screamed, 'And take your.........bull out of here.   A fine bill for damages you will haf to pay!'   But Eachann, quite composed, settled more comfortably on the folding chair and took his time over refilling his pipe.

'Inteet,' he remarked after a while to his fuming audience, once his pipe was drawing to his satisfaction, 'I am not surprised the poor beast iss annoyed the way you were all making a fool of her.'   He paused, ignoring the mounting tension as the noise reached a peak outside. 'Of coorse, maybe is iss not too late for the chudches to be having another look at her. Maybe if she saw the rosette for champion on her horns it would help.'

'Are you trying to suggest we should make that terrible beast the champion?' snarled the Chairman. 'Well, now,' replied Eachann with a look of surprised gratification on his face, 'That iss very kind of you to be saying it, but I am sure the chudches will be happy to agree.'

The Chairman, Committee and judges began to argue and shout until they nearly came to blows, but at length the Chairman came back to Eachann. 'Aal right,' he cried, his face all red and bursting with rage, 'You are nothing but a tirty thief. Yess, we'll make your ploddy pull the champion, BUT GET HER OUT OF HERE!'

'And that iss a fine silver cup you haf,' ruminated Eachann, 'And they say there iss fifteen pounds to go with it. Of coorse, you will be remembering the red cards and the class prizes ass well?'

'YESS, YESS, YESS, tam you,' screamed the Chairman, nearly snapping his cromag between his fingers with the rage that was on him.

'And ther will be no damaches to pay after aal?' persisted Eachann.

'N DIAOUL,' roared the poor man, nearly past caring, 'Chust take your pull and yourself out of here and you can haf what you like!'

So Eachann leisurely put away his pipe, finished the last of his dram, wipes his moustache, picked up his stick and strolled leisurely out of the tent, whistling under his breath his favourite pipe tune — *'Samuel the Weaver'*— with the whole crowd of officials jumping up and down, swearing and crowding at his back.

Just as they came round the corner, along came the bull making for the main road with half a marquee trailing behind and its back more like a line of washing than ever, for it was beginning to get somewhat tired. But when it saw Eachann it drew up so fast that its hooves scored the turf for twenty feet with the way that was on it. The bull mooed gently, came trotting up, and snuffed down Eachann's neck with every sign of pleasure.

Eachann put a halter on the beast out of his pocket, for it was never needed — just to reassure the terrified officials. He then led the bull up to the President, the Marquis of Mingary himself, that was a MacKinnon on his mother's side. The Secretary, with a dirty look at Eachann, came rushing forward with the prizes and the Marquis shook Eachann vaguely by the hand as he presented him with the rosettes, red cards, prizes and all. He couldn't tell a prize beast from a twelve-pointer on the hill, for he lived in London nearly all the time. As he had just reached the field to present the prizes, he probably thought the showground always looked like that; anyway, he beamed all round and looked very pleased with everything.

So home went Eachann and his bull, with a total of twenty-five pounds in prize money, two bottles of whisky, three pairs of braces, a cheese, and of course the silver cup: every prize he and the bull could possibly have won. It was the next year they altered the rules of the Show so that all exhibits were to be judged tied up in their stalls and pens, yes, even the poultry. That was the only way they could entice a judge to come back to the show.

TRAGEDY ROCK

TRAGEDY ROCK

The most spectacular stretch of road in Mull is where the coast road on the western seaboard winds along under the forbidding, crumbling 1,000 feet basaltic cliffs of Gribun.   Here the road is jammed precariously between the steep rocky glacis and the dangerous drop to the sea below, and is sometimes closed by rockfalls after frost or heavy rain — a half mile of road I am always happy to leave behind me   Westwards, with the island of Inch Kenneth off-shore, an island sacred in sanctity like Iona, the cliffs draw back leaving a strip of good arable land above the rocky shore, with a few houses and two farms.   The precipices are deeply eroded in places into chimneys down which little streams fall like narrow white veils, and are checked and blown back like smoke over their rim by Atlantic gales until the whole headland seems to be on fire.   It is a fit setting for the sad story of a young couple who perished there at Gribun on their wedding night.

Across the road from the first little farmhouse you come to, with a clump of wind-blown elder trees at the gable, you will see a huge boulder poised behind the fragments of a low stone wall.   It is known as *Clach-na-Lanain* or the Stone of the Couple.   A few yards above it is the face of a large outcrop of rock, and on either side you will see rocks and boulders deflected by the formation in their fall from the cliffs above.   There are several local versions of the story, but here are the facts, as told by the late Archie MacFadyen, whose family worked this farm for generations.

It was during the third week of September, and the harvest was almost secured, about the year 1700 — give or take a year or two — that a young man whose first name was John came from the island of Erraid (David Balfour's island in *Kidnapped*), just across from Iona, to take up duties as shepherd at Gribun.   He was engaged to marry a local girl, said to be Rona, daughter of the local blacksmith, and the wedding took place on the day he arrived, or the day after.   They had been fortunate in obtaining the tenancy of the convenient little one-roomed cot house that stood opposite the farmhouse in the shelter of the great rockface.   The celebrations and dance that followed the wedding were held in the barn just across the road, and continued until dawn.

Now, the day of the wedding had been threatening, with dark clouds building up, and through the night the storm broke, with the wind howling through the clefts of the cliffs and the rain coming down in sheets.   With the noise of the storm, the dancing, singing and the bagpipes, nobody heard the dreadful noise in the night as the great rock split, half of it rolling down the few intervening yards and coming to rest on top of the flattened cot house.   In it were the young couple, who had slipped away in the middle of the celebrations.   Archie MacFadyen told me how his grandmother used to describe how during her lifetime the ends of some of the rafters could still be seen projecting from under the boulder.

The unfortunate young couple were never seen again.   They lie beneath that great natural tomb; and in what was a tiny strip of garden behind the wall, flowers still spring up to their memory.

TRIALS OF STRENGTH

TRIALS OF STRENGTH

In the old days, members of the Clan Macnab were famous for their physical strength. Perhaps the most redoubtable of them all were the twelve sons of Finlay, the twelfth chief, back in the days of Montrose, two by his first wife, and ten by his second, the weakest of whom, it is said, could drive his dirk through a two-inch thick board. The oldest, Ian Min (*Smooth John* — a hirsute giant of a man), was particularly feared. He it was who with three of his brothers carried a boat over the hills from Loch Tay to Loch Earn one night in late December and rowed out to Neish Island, off St. Fillan's. Here the Clan Neish had collected every boat on Loch Earn, and thinking themselves secure in their island castle, they were feasting and drinking with the winter's provisions stolen earlier from a party of Macnabs conveying the stores peacefully to their stronghold on Eilean Ran on Loch Tay.

The four Macnab brothers broke into the Neish stronghold and put every one to the sword, missing only two children who had been covered up by some overturned furnishings. Afterwards Ian Min and his little party rowed back and began to carry the boat back to Loch Tay, but gave up near the summit, where the boat lay disintegrating for two centuries. Arriving home at the Macnab stronghold, they threw a sack containing the heads of some of the Neishes at the feet of their old father in proof of their prowess.

This was the episode that gave the Macnab's the Boat and Savage's head in their Coat of Arms. The Macnabs never contend — like the MacNeils and many other clans — that the boat in their Coat Of Arms commemorates the rival boat they had at the time of the Flood!

Ian Min was described in his day as *'The Great Montrossian'*, and he was indeed a tower of strength at the Battle of Kilsyth. Appointed garrison commander of Montrose's own castle of Kincardine in 1641, he held out successfully with 300 followers against the experienced troops of General Leslie, until being rduced to dire straits through lack of water and food, Ian Min staged a night sortie through the enemy lines with such success that his force escaped: only he himself and his servant, bringing up the rear, were captured. Sent to Edinburgh Castle and condemned to death, he escaped the night before his execution.

Defeated at Worcester in 1651 with the sad loss of many of his men, Ian Min escaped and returned home safely. However, a secret meeting of the supporters of Montrose was held at Killin, in Ian's home country, in 1653, but suspicions were raised in official circles and a party of troops was sent from Perth to investigate. When he discovered that these soldiers were lifting cattle locally, he set about them, but, alas, he was killed in the affray, thus ending the life of the most heroic figure in the Macnab house of Bovain.

Just 100 years later another powerful Macnab featured in a more humorous incident. This was Donald, second son of John, in Acharn, Glendochart. Born in 1715, he entered the army at the age of eighteen, but in 1741 gave it up and returned to civilian life. However, he joined the army of Charles Edward Stuart in the '45, and his great strength, added to his military training, did much to carry the day at the battle of Falkirk. Escaping after Culloden, and a wanted man, he took refuge in the fastnesses of Ben Cruachan, where his wants were looked after by his kinsmen, the workers in iron and armour at Barr a'Chaistelain, Dalmally.

Sometimes he ventured far afield incognito. One day, chancing to visit his house in Brae Leny, he was surprised by a party of redcoats, the hated *Saighdearean Dearg*, who were searching for him. Slipping out of a back window in a great rage, he picked up a baulk of timber, and coming round the gable end of the house he leaped at the soldiers guarding the front door and smashed two of them to death before making good his escape. Proscribed now as 'Donald Macnab, of Braeleing', he continued to move around the country, although with great circumspection.

One day, however, as he was mixing with the crowd at a public fair in Doune, he was accosted by a big, powerful sergeant from the garrison at Stirling, who, with a party of soldiers, had been deputised to arrest one Donald Macnab who had been reported as likely to be at the fair.

'What's yer name?' barked the sergeant suspiciously, eyeing him up and down. 'Is it Macnab?'

'Ach, no,' replied Donald mildly, 'I am a Campbell.' (While this was not strictly true, there were indeed matrimonial ties between the two clans.)

Mollified by the name Campbell, a clan usually safely on the side of established government, the sergeant returned: 'Just as well for you. We're looking for a rascal called Donald Macnab; in fact my captain will give a bright new golden guinea piece to lay hands on him. Ye'll earn that if ye tell me where he is.'

Donald appeared to turn this over in his mind, then looking round as furtively as any informer, he whispered in the ear of the sergeant. 'Meet me in the inn at sunset for a drink and I'll put Donald Macnab in your hands. I ken the man fine.'

At dusk the sergeant eagerly entered the inn, leaving a file of redcoats on guard outside. On seeing him, Donald waved him over to a seat and called for drinks.

'Well, Campbell,' said the soldier, 'Where's our Donald Macnab?'

'Wheest,wheest,' replied the other, 'There's plenty of time. First of all let's have our drink. Now, in Scotland we have a custom where we stand up and shake hands before our first drink. I'm sure you will join me — so here's to your good health.'

So saying he rose and extended his right hand to the unsuspecting sergeant, who found himself held in a vice-like grip.

'Now,' snarled the Macnab, 'I promised that you would lay hands on Donald Macnab; I am keeping my promise, for I am Donald Macnab — and this is what you get for asking a Highlander to betray a friend for your dirty gold.' He gave one mighty squeeze which crushed and snapped the bones in the sergeant's hand, so that the blood came oozing out.

Suddenly releasing his grip, Donald calmly drained the glass of *uisge beatha* in front of him, turned and marched through the not unsympathetic onlookers, past the soldiers waiting outside the door and to freedom, leaving the poor sergeant speechlessly clasping his mutilated hand under his oxter and weeping with pain and mortification.

Under the general amnesty, Donald was able to return later to enjoy his quiet life among the hills.

ESCAPE FROM A KILLER WHALE

ESCAPE
FROM A
KILLER WHALE

Once in a while we hear of the deaths or disappearance of inshore fishermen in the Hebrides.   Perhaps a body is recovered, or the lobster or salmon boat found wrecked or badly damaged.   It can be tragic, and often there is no rational explanation for the incident.   An experience in the north of Mull may explain something, at least, of the mystery.

Donnie is a quiet knowledgable islander, retired now, who during the season used to act as right-hand man for a local salmon fisher.   Among the duties were inspecting and maintaining the nets staked along a stretch of the coast.   These nets are twelve feet deep, stretched vertically by floats along the top or 'leader' rope, and weighted along the foot rope between two tall vertical posts anchored at the foot to the sea bed.   They are set at right angles to the coastal paths followed by the salmon, which, seeking a way around the net, enter a vertical one-way slit leading into the 'bag' where they are trapped, and from which they are removed daily.

In order to avoid the long journey to his home across the island, Donnie often stayed for days at a time in the cosy hut and store beside the inlet where the boat was tied up.   This was five miles from the village over a track negotiable only by a Land Rover.   A lover of nature, time did not hang heavily on Donnie's hands, what with fishing off the rocks, bird watching and keeping an eye on the nets. Seals, in particular, can seriously affect the livelihood of the salmon fisher by tearing valuable nets beyond repair to get at the salmon, which escape through the rents, or are eaten, or mangled and left unsaleable. Donnie, a crack shot, used to watch out for seals and scare them off. Seals have their place, but not to increase in numbers that interfere with the economics of fishermen. Basking sharks sometimes were tangled up in a net, but by accident, as they are harmless plankton eaters.

I once asked Donnie if he had ever been in a tight corner in the course of his fishing career, and he described how he had had the fright of his life one day when he was on his own and out inspecting the nets.

It was a calm, sunny day, he said, and the nets were fairly close in. He decided to row out in the small dinghy to check them over. He had just reached the leader of one of the nets and was looking down at one or two salmon flashing about in the bag when he noticed the big dorsal fins of some large fish some distance out cutting through the water and moving steadily towards him. The approach was more like that of a pair of Orca, or killer whales — more decisive than that of a basking shark. He kept the dinghy close to the net as he watched the fish (or were they mammals?) coming nearer and nearer, until suddenly the fins disappeared, and down in the clear water he saw the twenty foot shape of a killer whale slanting up at him with its mouth open and showing its murderous teeth.

Donnie realised the danger he was in, and wondered if he was going to finish up as another victim in a local mystery, for the brute could snap the dinghy in halves and himself along with it. In desperation he gave a heave at the oars and bumped the boat across the leader where it dipped between two floats, and crossed to the other side of the net.

The killer shot to the surface with its mouth gaping, but stopped sharply when confronted by the net, which it seemed to mistrust. It hung there in the water staring up at the boat, seemingly to work out a logical solution for attack. Then as if it had come to a decision, it whipped round, shot out to sea, and came speeding back round the other side of the net. Again Donnie heaved the boat across the leader to his original side, and again the killer drew up sharply at the net. By great good luck the other killer whale took no part in the performance. For a third time the brute repeated the tactic, and Donnie was again saved by the net. This time, however, it seemed to tire of its efforts to trap the man and after staring up through the net for some time it slowly drifted away out of sight. Presently it appeared to have been joined by its consort, and the two big fins could be seen again moving away along the open sea beyond the cliffs. Donnie waited there for fully half an hour in case the cunning creatures would come back. At last he took to the oars and returned to the safety of his shore base just as hard as he could row.

Donnie was lucky. How many unfortunate men have vanished over the years in similar circumstances?

TALES TOLD BY

DO'L GORM

DO'L GORM HOLDS THE LINE

Snug under the sheltering overhang of the roadside quarry, where Do'l Gorm had erected a contraption of corrugated iron sheets, we listened to the sough of the wind in the double row of telephone wires above us. I had been driven off the loch, now streaked with lines of foam, by a raging gale that had suddenly sprung up. I was in no hurry. The wind would blow me on my bicycle the four miles to my home in a few minutes almost without touching the pedals. The shelter creaked rustily. On a turf seat beside me, Do'l Gorm alternately gurgled at his pipe and raised his cracked voice in a lugubrious rendering of '*Farewell to Fuinary*', whose opening lines belie its inherent sadness:-

'*The day wass good, the breese wass fine*
Ass we sped swuftly o'er the brine.....'

Presently he broke off and glanced up reflectively at the telephone wires. 'It iss a wee bit like the day Lachie's sheep broke into Katie Crupach's croft,' he began. 'The time they cleaned out nearly aal her young crops. I mind the day fine, because it wass the only time I effer tried my hand at the tellyphone. A stupid thing; I don't know how anybody can be bothered with it.' Do'l Gorm prepared to dismiss the subject with an expressive shrug of utter contempt.

'Yess,' he added, 'There iss a lot to be said for the old days. No motor cars to keep breaking up the roads a man has to keep mending with his sore back; no wireless to keep him up half the night; no Pos-toffice with its bills and Income Tax letters. That Income Tax,' he continued malevolently, 'I mind one woman that lived in the town with a lot of money. The Income Tax man at Dunoon got to hear about her and sent her a letter. Of coorse she never knew what he wass talking about, so she sat down and wrote back pretty sharp and never put a stamp on her letter. She said:- "I do not want to join your Income Tax, for I have been with the Prudential since it started up at Calamore, and I am not going to change now." Wassn't that smart of her? It fairly sorted the Income Tax man anyway.'

'But wait you, now,' I broke in, 'About the telephone. You must admit it has its good points. What about the fire at Glenbuie yon Saturday night — the way the Calamore Fire Brigade got on the job when the telephone call came through?'

'Ach, yess,' retorted the roadman cynically, 'And what did they do anyway? By the time they got the team together from the Galleon Bar and the Maclean Arms, and knocked up Mackenzie the Garage to get the battery for the lorry, there wass nothing left by the fire except the stables.'

'But you know fine it was because they ran out of petrol on the Bealach Dubh hill that they were late. Anyway, what about the time Archie the Keeper fell over the rocks at Craig a Chait and broke his leg, how fast the doctor got the ambulance when he telephoned?'

'Hach, better if Archie the Keeper broke his neck,' growled Do'l Gorm, for the keeper was inclined to cramp some of his less publicised activities.

'Well, now,' I prompted gently, 'What was yon about Lachie's sheep?'

'Ho, yess, I wass just going to tell you about it. Stop you till I get my pipe going.' Having stuffed his pipe with about an ounce of a revolting substance shaved from a black plug and ground down between leathery palms, he lit up in a manner reminiscent of the French expression *Allumer du feu.*

'It wass when the tellyphone had just come to the island and one of the first boxes wass set up at the Eas Crossroads, its new pent red and shining, and ther wass still glass in most of the windows. It wass a wild day chust like this and I wass on my way up to the Bealach here ass usual when I saw Lachie's sheep — a whole flock of them — running through the gate into Katie Crupach's croft and starting to eat her young turnips. That iss the worst of putting up an old bedstead for a gate — there's no way to hang it, and fine the young beasts know. Of coorse, Lachie's sheep should not haff been loose on the road; but he had been putting off mending the dyke of his own croft that fell down the winter before, and the wind blew down the dead fir tree he had lifted from the Forestry to fill the space. It was no use me trying to shift the sheep once they had the taste. Only a dog would do it. All right, I said to maself, I wonder can I give Lachie a tellyphone to save me walking back down the hill. Maybe he will be up by now. So I made for the box.

'There was that much glass round it I had a chob to find the door, and I wass wild when the tam thing snapped shut on my fingers. But I was inside. There wass a shelf with a big book below it and a money box fixed hard down, maybe for donations to the Pos-toffice. There wass two kinds of black handles sitting on the top, so I picked them up the way I wass seeing in the picture papers and put my mouth to speak in one of them. But before I could say a word, a very polite voice away in the distance began to say: "Number Please?"

'I knew at once it would be the gyurl from Glasgow with the paper shoes and pin heels that wass on loan to learn Flora

McVouran in the Pos-toffice how to work the tellyphone. You would laugh at the way aal the young fellows in Calamore wass after her to go for a walk through the woods or round by the point. At first the only one she would go with wass Peter the Goat, a fine-looking chap right enough, for his father wass Calum a'Sgiobair —you know, the lobster fisher. But the heels was right off her shoes in the first mile or two — before they wass right started — and he had to hold her up aal the way home. Anyway, that wass their story for the long time they wass away.

'But what wass I telling you ? — Oh, yess: "Number please," she wass saying. Now, chust at first I thought to maself that wass right smart of her to guess what wass wrong, so I called to her: "Now chust you stop a minute and I'll count." I had to shout pretty hard to make her hear, but of coorse the Pos-toffice iss a long distance away. Then I heard her call out to speak the number into the other black handle, and it wass easier after that.

'"Ther will be about eighteen," I says to her.

'"Do you mean Calamore one-eight," she raps back at me, and before I could tell her it wassn't Calamore or yet Achamore that I wass wanting, I hears a new voice: "Hello? Who is it?" in one of those accents you hear on the twelfth of August when London iss empty.

' "It's maself," I replies as pleasant as I could. "Iss Lachie there?" — but she cuts in quick — "Ther iss nobody of that name here. This iss Colonel Bulmer-Brown's residence." — that's old Bloomers Brown, you know, that used to take the Big House effery summer.

'Tach, I couldn't make out what wass going on; but after a bit the English "Hellos" stopped, and the gyurl began her "Number please?" once again.

' "Am I not trying to tell you," I snaps back pretty short. "Ther iss eighteen in Katie Crupach's croft — no, stop you a minute —

twenty three. Ther iss other five running in. I haf got to speak to Lachie."

' "I don't know what you are talking about," she speaks back. "Just what number DO you want?"

' "I am not wanting any number at aal," I shouted: "Twenty three iss far too many ass it is. I chust want to say to Lachie that if he doesn't get up here fast with the dog ther will be nothing left of Katie Crupach's crops."

' "What on earth are you talking about?" says the gyurl, chust ass if I wass a fool.

' "Amn't I telling you" — and I wass real mad — "It iss about the sheep that hass broken into Katie Crupach's croft—"

'Ther wass a buzzing of voices on the tellyphone like the day my bees swarmed into the manse tea-party, and I wass chust going to throw down the tam machine and clear out when I heard Flora McVouran's voice speaking quietly in my ear.

' "Wass you wanting to speak to Lachie Thomson?" she says. "Well, he hass not got the tellyphone, but if it iss important I''ll chust run over to the house and give him a message."

'So I explained it aal to her and she told me to hang up the handles when I wass done. Such an obliching, sensible gyurl! So I did that and went out, but that tam door snapped shut again on my fingers when I tried to close it.

'By this time aal the turnips wass gone; but ther wass plenty of young corn to keep the sheep going until Lachie came peching up with that useless black and white collie of his. If only I had gone down the road for him at the start we might haf saved the crops. Oh, I wass right sorry for her.

'Yess,' concluded Do'l Gorm with sincere conviction, 'Maybe the tellyphone iss good for some folks, and cheap too, for I'm sure there wouldn't be many people putting any donations in the box. But I neffer touched the thing again in my life.'

At this point the wind and rain began to ease off, so I took the chance to mount my bicycle and head for home.   In my ears the moaning of the wind was a fitting accompaniment to the receding finale of:-

'Farewell, farewell to Fuinary'

— which sounded even more melancholy the way Do'l Gorm sang it.

SNAKES AND ADDERS

SNAKES AND ADDERS

When I jumped off my bicycle at the quarry one hot August day for a welcome drink at the ice-cold spring and a talk with the old roadman, I saw I had been forestalled.   Two hikers had come to a halt, seemingly as Do'l Gorm was in the middle of his fire-raising ceremony, apparently fascinated by the performance.   He, in turn, was arrested by the remarkable sight in front of him, so much so that the match burned out unheeded between his fingers and his pipe drooped among his whiskers.

That the figures were male and female there could be little doubt.   The ample and uninhibited curves of the one were no less unmistakeable than the thin shanks and straggling, ill-nurtured beard of the other.   One thing was common to both — the long expanses of white and unprotected limbs, and the bulky rucksacks, which indicated that they had come from the big city and just arrived on the island.

Almost unheeded I lowered myself thankfully on to the shaded grassy bank beside them and prepared to listen.   I was sure there was rich material here on which Do'l Gorm could hone his wit.   Seemingly I had just missed a leading question, for Do'l Gorm with an obvious effort directed his mild blue eyes to a more general contemplation of his audience.

'You wass asking if there iss serpents on the island,' he began. 'My chove,' he added enthusiastically, as if he was entertaining two keen zoologists, 'You couldn't haf come to a better place.'

The two strangers glanced at each other and round about with some apprehension and moved away from the rich growth of heather and bracken to the more open floor of the quarry.

'Why,' continued the raconteur, 'This ferry glen iss called the *Bealach Naithir* — what you would say in English Snake Pass. Of coorse, there iss not ass many now as when I wass a young man. Ther iss a place along the road here where you are going that used to be infested with serpents, not one of them shorter than my stick. You will likely see plenty of them yet. I haf drove a horse and cart on a day like this and effery wee while I would be leaning over with a spade to clear them off the wheels before the axle jammed solid. They wass sleeping in the dust of the road in the hot sun, layers and layers of them.

'Did you say "What about the horse?" Hach, you must understand that Mull horses iss stung so much with serpents they become in tune to the poison and the serpents know it iss chust a waste of time to sting them anymore.

'You see the size of Loch Caman Amais down ther? Well, when the serpents became thirsty, so many would be crowding down to the edge for a drink they had to queue up.

'What wass you saying? Did I see any slow-worms among them? Chust let me tell you that the only time a Mull worm iss slow is when it iss waiting on a hook to grip a trout. But it iss serpents I wass talking about — now, ther's a thing, the way they milk the cows — they love the milk, you see. Stop you and I'll tell you a story about that.

'You wouldn't know Duncan Flora. His right name wass Maclean, but ther wass so many Macleans that efferybody called him Duncan Flora because of his mother. Well, he wass the best man at a bargain that effer went to Oban market. One day he came home with two cows, the thinnest you effer saw. He must have picked them up as rechects. He kept them in the old byre up at his croft and effery morning let them loose on the Big Hill wher the grazings iss free. Maybe he didn't as much drive ass help them up the road, for many's the time the poor beasts had to lean against the dyke for support when Duncan stopped for a crack with somebody. I used to make fun of them, but he would haf none of it.

' "They are champion mulkers," he claimed. "It iss not their fault if I only get a wee chug of milk from them at night. It iss because of the serpents."

' "Iss that so," I said to him, "And what would the serpents be haffing to do with the mulk?"

' "Little you know," replied Duncan, quite sharp. "It wass one afternoon last month I found out for maself. It wass in the hot weather after the Glasgow Fair Floods, when I went looking for them to bring them home. And what do you think? When I got near enough I saw four serpents ass long ass my arm sitting on their tails under each cow and sucking away at the mulk ass hard ass they could go. I shouted at them and waved my stick, but they neffer bothered. What wass worse, a whole crowd more of them waiting their turn lifted their heads above the heather and hissed at me. I can tell you, I ran for my life. Effer since I chust let the cows come home themselves when they are ready."

'Well, Duncan told the story so often that people began to believe him. The serpents neffer seemed to touch any other beast on the hill, but of coorse they didn't often go to the wee glen wher he said he saw them being mulked. When the Autumn sales came round, Duncan wass to sell his two cows that wass looking thinner than effer, if that wass possible. He assured strangers that these fine animals, if kept away from the serpents, would give gallons of good mulk; and of coorse, any of his friends that wass near would back up the story. Some buyer must haf been interested, for Duncan came home with a pocket full of money and a smile on his face ass wide ass this quarry.

' "I came well out of that deal," he told me next time we met. "Do you know, a man from Bunessan gave me £12:10s. for the two cows." I would say maself that Duncan Flora must haf made at least £12 on the deal! But wait you!

'At the Salen Show next year I got on the crack with a man from Bunessan. He asked me if I knew a Duncan Maclean in Calamore, the man he bought two cows off last year. "You will be meaning Duncan Flora," I said to him, and to maself I wass thinking — "Now for it; a good chob Duncan iss not here at the Show."

' "Well," the man said, "I'll tell you something about those cows. When I got home with them to Bunessan I put them in the field next to the house where we could keep an eye on them and chase away the serpents, chust like Duncan told me to do. My, these serpents up there must be the fair duvvle. Do you know, in a few weeks these cows wass chust ass fat and sleek ass effer you saw. In fact, one took a prize for champion mulker. I haf chust been offered £40 for her, but no fear! I wouldn't part with these cows, no, not for all the gold in the Spanish Armada!" '

Pale, but not loitering, the two hikers hitched their packs, gave us a hasty word of departure and took the road. They were last seen mincing delicately down the exact centre of the road in single file, their eyes feverishly searching every tuft of heather and frond of bracken along the verges likely to conceal units of a deadly army of six-foot adders!

THE LOBSTER OF CALIACH

THE LOBSTER OF CALIACH

The breeeze had gone down and the trout with it.   Unbroken by
the dimple of a single rising fish, the surface mirrored the bracken,
heather and birch trees and the bald rocks that crowned the steep
hill on the other side of the Loch.   I reeled in, hitched my bag, and
strolled up the rough path through the bracken, breathing the
unforgettable scents of wild mint and bog myrtle from the margins
of the loch.   In front of the quarry above me, Angus More's float
was drawn up, the horse cropping the grass along the edge of the
ditch.   No wonder the horse welcomed a break.   Angus ran the
local transport and some of the loads were fair killers on the steep
hills out of Calamore.

Do'l Gorm peered over the edge of the float as I came and passed
the time of day.   He pointed his pipe distastefully at the few boxes
of fine lobsters which Angus was hurrying in to catch the afternoon
boat for the south.

'These will be from Archie over at Dun-a'Bhan,' he remarked,
examining the name on the labels.   'Poor stuff,' he scoffed,
turning his back contemptuously on the offending crustaceans.
'They are that small now-a-days there iss nothin on them but a
taste.   I would ass soon have a plate of dulse or carrageen.

'Now, when I wass young, we had real lobsters.   The ones that
lived in the tangles under the cliffs by Ardmore and Caliach.   One
of them would need a box aal to himself, maybe made to

77

measure. Yess, that iss what spoilt the fishing. Wood was that scarce and dear and freight so high it didn't pay them any more. But before that I haf seen the Bay so full of lobster boxes waiting to be lifted the boat could hardly get into the pier and ther wass no room for the yats to anchor. When one of these lobsters wass put in the window of the fish shops in Glasgow — if there was room — nobody would believe, and they wass running into the nearest pub for another haff to see if it would put away the vision.

'But stop you and I'll tell you about the biggest lobster of all — you will be in plenty of time for the boat, Angus.

'You would be hearing of the big liner *Aurania* that went down in 1916 right against the cliff at Caliach after drifting all the way from Islay, where she wass mined, and they had no tugs handy to try to save her. A wild place, Caliach, with the waves straight from America and yon nasty tide rip chust off the Point. Well, after a while the lobsters began to come in about the hull — they are very fond of old wrecks — big ones, too, and aal red with rust. Yess, that iss one kind of red lobster that wass alive aal right!

'At that time I wass helping the MacDonalds with their lobster boat; they wass always losing creels about the wreck, even in fine weather, but they kept on for the sake of the fine catches in the ones that wass left.

'It wass chust after the end of the war the salvage ship came along with a diver to try and get the safe out of the captain's cabin. Seeing I knew chust exactly how she wass lying, I got a chob on the salvage boat to show them. It wass a long time for once of fine, calm, summer weather and we had the ship moored in no time at all.

'Well, the first time the diver went down the MacDonalds wass busy lifting their creels beside us, cursing away something terrible at the way nearly aal the creels wass gone that day, clean off the ropes. He wass chust letting down one or two spare ones full of bait when the diver chugged his rope to be brought up. He was aal excited. When they unscrewed the helmet he said that there wass the father of aal lobsters down ther inside the ship reaching out its claws through the hole wher she was mined, and champing down the bait, creels and aal.

'The captain cocked his ears at this. "Come on," he called, chust for a joke, "Let's haf a record lobster for tea!" So they made a snare like a big rabbit snare with heavy wire hawser and lowered it from the derrick with the diver guiding them until it wass chust in front of the hole. Then the MacDonalds let down another creel filled to the top with bait, chust out from the snare. Right enough, out came the head and claws of a chiant lobster. The diver gave the signal, the crew started up the winch, and the snare tightened up, gripping the lobster right behind the claws.

'But they couldn't move it. In fact, it pulled back into the wreck. They shifted the hawser to the strongest lifting winch on the ship and started it going; the strain got more and more until the salvage ship began to heel over, and the captain screamed at them to slacken off or the whole ship would be coped. But he was a stubborn man, and he had his pride. This fine ship of his wouldn't be beat by any lobster, not even a record one. He tried effery trick of the trade but nothing would budge it but dy-namite, and he was afraid to use that in case he lost the safe that he remembered chust in time wass down in the captain's cabin, and it wass the safe and not the lobster he wass supposed to be getting.

'He sent the mate over to the Pos-toffice to tellyphone — no, it wass the telegraph; that wass before the tellyphone came in — to send up a couple of yon big caymels from Liverpool; that iss the big tanks they use for lufting submarines from the bottom. A few days later they came alongside ass fast ass the tugs could bring them.

'The crew — who had been enchoying the rest, fishing and sunbathing and trips to Lachie's place in the village (they wass a thirsty lot, and nearly cleaned him out of his stocks) — had to get busy again.   The caymels wass sunk beside the hull of the wreck and the hawser shifted on to them from the winches.   Then they began to pump in the air.   Man, after a bit it wass like the Day of Chudgement.   Bubbles and old timbers came up.   The sea wass boiling and the ferry cliffs began to shake with the strain.   Then ther came a crash like a depth charge going off below, and up came the caymels, pumped dry, and lashed between them wass the most chiant lobster you effer saw!   Man, it wass a whopper!   But stop you: it wass not the lobster that had let go, but the hull of the *Aurania* that had given way, for under the tail of the lobster wass still clamped one of the ship's boilers with aal the steam pipes snapped off and hanging loose: but here's the thing — in its front claws the poor wise beast wass holding up the captain's safe from down below to make peace with us!

'Well, what could we do?   We chust let down the grab and took the safe from it and cut the poor beast free from the hawser and let it go back down none the worse.   Maybe it is still ther to this day.   Anyway, the MacDonalds neffer lost another creel ther.'

Do'l Gorm coughed complacently, seated himself on the grassy bank and directed his gaze into the middle distance as he began to fill his pipe.   Just at that the urgent bleat of a distant ship's siren recalled Angus More to an awareness of his duties.   With hardly time for a Gaelic valediction he rocketed away down the road with his startled horse going flat out over the pot-holes left, even enlarged, by Do'l Gorm for the discomfort of the new motor post-van, his pet aversion.

Thoughtfully and more sedately I took the road for home.

A DROP OF THE HARD STUFF

A DROP OF THE HARD STUFF

The first of January came in dry, calm, and — appropriately enough — with a nip in the air.   About noon, when the village was coming to life again, I picked my way with perhaps over-elaborate care through the ranks of 'Dead Marines' which stood, lay, or spread themselves in clinking fragments in the neighbourhood of the Galleon Inn and the Maclean Arms.   As usual, Do'l Gorm was waiting for my ceremonial visit with everything in readiness. He had a gay new cloth on the table on which were set a big square bottle, two tumblers and a wee box of shortbread.   The house was even more spotless than usual, for although he lived by himself (some day I'll tell you why he never married), his pride in the trim little place would have put many a house-proud woman to shame.

We observed the ceremonial shaking of hands and exchanged apropriate salutations in all sincerity.   I passed over my gift, a cylindrical parcel whose seductive *'glooping'* sound left no doubts as to its nature.   My friend received it with his customary air of surprised reluctance which deceived neither of us, and placed it on the dresser with a reverence equalled only by his bosom friend Lachie with the Church plate on Sundays.

After a while, Do'l Gorm wiped his moustache with a fine sweeping gesture and held his tumbler up to the light with the studied criticism of a connoiseur.

'Well, now,' he remarked, 'Considering that the days of water-proof whisky iss past, this stuff iss no' so bad at aal. No' so bad. Stop you and I'll fill them up again.'

After another exchange of *'Slainte Mor'* we relaxed in our chairs, nibbling a fragment of shortbread to restore our palates to a state of balanced appreciation. Into Do'l Gorm's eyes there came that happy, far-away gleam which heralded another tale from his inexhaustible store of reminiscences.

'I mind fine,' he began, 'When they used to make it along ther at the disillery, just below the East Brae. It is a garridge now wher it iss only spirits for the motors they are keeping. Man, those were the days! Ther wass no unemployment in Calamore then when the whisky wass working. Effery able-bodied man had plenty to do inside, or cutting and working the peats on the hill and bringing them to the distillery by the cartload. I had a steady chob myself in the still room — many's the ploy we had!

'I could neffer stand more than a cupful of it myself, but some of the old hands could be drinking the neat spirits by the pint ass it came off the still, chust like it wass water. Of coorse, we had to be very careful how we did it, for you can be sure we wass well watched. But it wass when we had to go into the bonded store to shift the casks, man, that wass when we tasted the real stuff. Of coorse, the gauger would be with us aal the time, but it wass enough to draw his attention to something chust long enough for us to get busy at the other side putting a gimlet under a cask. A wee plug of wood and a wipe of dust and nobody would effer know. When some of the casks wass broken up years later they wass like hedgehogs inside with the wooden plugs! It wass easy enough to hide a wee flat medicine bottle of spirits ass we came out.

'But talking about gaugers, I neffer told you about the ter I had once when I was on the distillery chob. I wass living then on my married sister — it wass her man wass the bow rope on the *Lochinvar*, with a wee croft up by the Achafraoch. Ther wass a byre ther away at the top corner beside the wood at the foot of the hill. Now, ther was an unusual demand for spirits in the island chust about then, so as the making of it was something I knew about, I began to think I would be haffing a go at making a wee still of my own. One bit at a time I got the pieces together and set them up at the far end of the byre wher there wass an old boiler with a chimney going up. I put up a good wall of hay and bracken for wintering the beasts right up to the roof until you would neffer guess ther was anything behind it but the back wall.

'The smock from the fire was a bother, and the smell, too. One dodge the gaugers used to haf was to go a distance and walk across the wind, sniffing like a pointer for the smell of the wash that would go for a mile downwind. Whenever he got it, all he had to do was walk up wind until the smell stopped — and ther wass the still. Fine I knew it would take a better man than the gauger we had to cross the bogs, climb the hill and fight through the trees in the wood with enough breath left in him for a sniff. And again, I neffer did the chob unless the wind wass blowing the smock through the trees and up the hill. Down at the village nobody bothered about me up at my sister's croft ass long ass I wass natural and didn't show ass if I wass working too hard. And, of coorse, seeing my clothes always had the smell of the distillery chob about them, that wass aal right too. It was safe enough.

'After a while I had quite a lot of whisky safely hidden away nice and convenient, and mind you, it tasted no' bad. I began to let my friends have a taste of it — chust for a small consideraation. If the bottle wass filled hard up to the cork ther would be no noise and nobody would know what wass wrapped up in the old newspapers. I got my sister's wee boy to take the bottles round the back doors late in the evenings. She thought it wass fish the boy wass delivering, for I would say to her I wass away up at the Lochs or out in the boat aal the time I wass at the Achafraoch.

'Efferything wass going chust fine, and I wass surprised the way

I wass gathering up a bit of money. In fact — between ourselfs — but for that money I could neffer haf manached to buy this fine wee house. But it aal had to end sometime; and that wass when the new gauger came to the place. He wass a keen man with a nose for trouble and a wife that wass terrible at the nagging. Maybe that accounted for him. Very soon he began to think ther wass something going on, even if he neffer felt it in the wind. Ther wass no proof at aal — until something happened that gave him that aal right! One evening the wee boy handed in one of the parcels at the gauger's back door instead of at the captain's next door. By good luck, the gauger's wife that came to the door didn't know the boy or get a look at his face and he was away like a shot. But when the parcel wass opened, then the ructions started.

'The gauger wass like a roaring lion. The first thing wass a notice offering £20 reward for information that would lead to the finding of a still in the district. Then the questionings for weeks and weeks — into efferything and effery corner — except the back of the byre at the Achafraoch.

'Of coorse, I wass one of the last people he would think of and my friends would neffer dream of saying a word. But, tach, after a while I said to myself it wass no use being greedy and keeping on risking it; so one dark night I slipped away up the back way to the croft. I poured the last of the wash down a hole and covered it in. Then I took the still to pieces. I packed the whole lot into sacks and carried them up to the old peat workings at the Lochs wher I buried them deep. It took the whole night and I wass dead beat in the morning, in fact I wass that stiff I could hardly go to work. But neffer mind, I wass aal in the clear.

'It would be a week or two later when the marks of my digging wass away that I took the gauger aside one day in the distillery and told him it had come to my ears ther wass a still buried in the peat near the lochs — but not to let on I told him. I didn't know whose it wass, or anything else except the place. In fact, maybe it wass chust a tale, but that wass what they wass saying. He wass very pleased and excited and told me to get a gang together next day and we would go for a search.

'It was chust like a holiday, even if we had to carry up the spades and crowbars. We had a free dinner out of a basket and a dram, and we manached to look busy until the afternoon. Of coorse, nobody but myself wass in the know, you must remember. Well, when it wass getting near time to go, I kind of encourached some of them to haf a try over wher I had planted the still, and the gauger came over with us. Poor man, I wass sorry for him, doing most of the work, sweating away in his shirt sleeves, prodding away in the peat with a crowbar with his hands aal blistered and himself covered with mud.

'Well, did one of the men not come on some of the metal at once, and wassn't the gauger pleased when the worm and the black pot and the pipes was lifted out of the bog! He gave each of us a pound note on the spot, and a few days later he handed me the £20 reward. Him and me wass chust like THAT! effer afterwards.

'After all, the still wass beginning to go done anyway, so maybe I didn't come out of it so bad in the end. When I bought this house soon afterwards I chust let word get round that it wass with some money left by an old uncle up at Aultbea. And seeing the mailboat didn't caal ther, ther wass no way they could prove anything else.'

A CASE OF SALVAGE

A CASE OF SALVAGE

The Old New Year is still observed in many corners of the Highlands and Islands; that is, of course, the true date on which the New Year comes in, despite those new-fangled changes which were made to the calendar. In any case, it is one date which can well stand being duplicated. Thanks to certain contacts of mine up Speyside, I can provide hospitality fitting to the occasion and aceptable to the true observers who drop in that evening.

Under an arrangement of long standing, Do'l Gorm reciprocates my visit to him on the 1st of January by looking in at my house on the 12th. On the occasion I have in mind, I can still see him sitting across from me in the other armchair with his eyes sparkling with eager anticipation of the half tumbler of pale amber fluid in front of him. After a decent interval he stirred, directed a shot of tobacco juice into the exact centre of the glowing birch logs (but apologetically, for Do'l Gorm knew his manners), stroked his whiskers with that fine, wide characteristic gesture of his, engulfed the tumbler in his hand and slowly drew in about half its contents.

'My chove,' he remarked appreciatively, smacking his chops and screwing up his eyes in enjoyment, 'I didn't know they were making stuff like that any more. Wher did you get it? — but, hach, that iss none of my business. Ass long ass we can get the ordinary stuff, we're no' so bad.'

'Was there ever a time you ran clean out of it?' I enquired, 'Sometime you couldn't even lay hands on a small sensation even for emergencies?'

'Well, mostly I manached,' he replied thoughtfully. 'It wass aal right at the South African war, but man, we wass gey short of it at times during the World War. In fact, that wass not long after the time I wass telling you about when I had the fun with the gauger. But I believe the worst time we effer had wass up at Sneebost. I'll chust tell you about that.

'I wass not on the roads aal my life. Well, this time I am telling you about happened a while before the Council invited me to take over the Bealach road out of Calamore, when I wass up with a small gang and a foreman mending Sneebost pier with a diver. Now, in those days ther was no hotel in Sneebost, and the place wass chust crawling with Wee Frees, U.Ps., F.Ps., and T.Ts. Man, if you dared to go for a walk on a Sunday you would be smelling the fire and brimstone with the looks you would be getting from yon black beetles going aal day between their houses and the kirk — and the bells ringing aal the time until you were near demented.

'After the first few days we hadn't a drop left except the foreman — and he kept his bottle locked up. Oh, he wass mean, mean. We got weaker and weaker until we could hardly turn the handles of the diver's air pump. However, one day the *Plover* — or wass it the *Dirk*? — came in with a mixed cargo to unload. Anyway, we had to stop work when she wass alongside. After a few hours, when the foreman saw the cargo wass nearly aal out, he thought we might lend a hand to the two pier hands. Now, ther wass a case of whisky for some place away across the island. Well, ass the sling around the case wass being raised, tam it if the man on the rope didn't lose his grip, the jib swung out and the case slupped out and went into the sea. Well, that wass that, and ther wass nothing we could do about it, so the *Plover* —no, no, I mind now (my memory iss going!) it was the *Dirk*, because wee Uisken wass bow rope — she cast off and moved on to Castlebay.

'Seeing it wass so late the foreman told us to pack up for the day, aal but the diver and the two pump hands (I wass one of them). He had a word with the diver and seemed to be explaining about some prochecting girder. "We can't leave it like that," he wass saying, "For if the fishing boats come alongside it could damach them. On you go — ten minutes will do the chob."

'Well, it wass me and Calum Ban on the pump. Calum wass one of these men with no imachination. Chust put a thing in his hand and he will be doing away at till next month unless you tell him — so we turned the handles and down went the diver. Now as I looked over the edge of the pier I saw a strange thing. The bubbles coming up from the diver wass going out from the pier instead of going out of sight under it. After a few minutes they came back in and up came the diver. "Well, boys," he says ass we were unscrewing his helmet, "That's fine. Efferything fixed now."

'You will know that although maybe I neffer say very much I think a lot. Aal right. I kept thinking of the foreman, the case of whisky and the diver, and I wondered if ther wass some private game going on. So at dark, when they wass aal settled for the night in the bothy, I went quietly down to the pier. The tide wass far out and ther wass nobody about except some scarts out on the rocks among the tangles. I felt my way down the iron rungs that wass set into one of the piles of the pier, and right enough, chust ass I thought, there wass the diver's rope tied to the bottom rung and going down into the water. I bent down, got a grip on it, and pulled: yess, ther wass something heavy on the other end. I pulled it to the surface and saw it wass the white wood of the case of whisky.

'Well, with a bit of a heave I got it up on the pier, and I sat down on a bollard to haf a smock while the water drained out. Then seeing ther wass still nobody about, I heaved the case on to my shoulder and picked my way along the shore among the rocks, wher I soon found a safe hole to hide it, and covered it up with loose stones.

'I slupped back into the bothy and nobody noticed I'd been out. Next day ther wass ructions. The diver and foreman were going at it until they wass nearly at blows, and what with efferybody being so dry and not knowing what it wass aal about ther wass nothing to do but work.

'But neffer you mind. One wet day later on, when the work wass near finished, I slupped away along the shore and manached to bring a load of bottles back to the bothy when they wass out. When the gang came in, ther wass a whole bottle of whisky at effery man's place, and his tin mug beside it, yess, even in front of the foreman. My chove, you should haf seen their faces! I don't remember much of what happened later, but the old folk of Sneebost still pull long faces and tell about that night to this ferry day.

'Of coorse, ther wass a bottle or two left over for myself — chust for a nip now and then when nobody wass looking — chust to keep out the cold wind. It was tam good whisky — I can nearly taste it yet!

'Well, well: *slainte mhath agus slainte mhor!'*

THE EELS OF MULL

THE EELS OF MULL

The July rainy period, or as we called it in Calamore, the
Glasgow Fair Floods (which mark the eagerly awaited coming of
the salmon and the seatrout) were almost over.   The streets were
wet and wind-swept, and the few holiday-makers who were not
indoors were lapped in waterproofs, seeking in the caress of the
mild rain a renewal of glowing complexions drained of their healthy
radiance by a year of city life.   It was Saturday night, and the bar
of the Maclean Arms was crowded.   In fact, there was even a
small overflow of strangers into the inner sanctum which Big
Duncan tried to reserve for his regulars.   Do'l Gorm, however,
with his usual diffident charm, had managed to insert himself into
his favourite seat and having reached the last half-inch of his first
glass he was casting a speculative eye on some of the types round
him.

On the other side of the table two men were arguing heatedly
over something appearing in the morning paper.

'Ach, its a' a bit of noansense,' exclaimed the one contemptuously.   'Ivery year yer Loch Ness Moanster comes oot jist
before the hoalidays.   Man, that's no coin-ceedence; its deliberate
poalicy by the Toorist Board!'

'Its noathin' o' the sort,' countered the other.   Pointing to the
paper which lay before them, he averred: 'Of coorse there's a
monster.   Photographs like this wan prove it: they have written
books about; why, even Saint Columba saw it awa' back in the
earliest times.'

'Havers!' cut in the first man.

'All, right; why is it only seen in the summer? Because it is either dormant in the winter, or it can't be seen because of wind and waves and darkness. Besides.....'

It was at this point I noticed a gleam of anticipation come into Do'l Gorm's eyes. As the second man paused for breath, the old man inserted a quiet verbal wedge into the argument.

'It iss a strange place, Loch Ness,' he observed mildly, 'And I am thinking the stories you are hearing could be right enough. Now, if it wass in the Island of Mull.....' Here he broke off, drained the last reluctant drops from his glass, set it down with exaggerated care, wiped his whiskers with that fine, wide gesture of his, and fixed his gaze on the "Old Mull" calendar issued by John Hopkins and Company fifteen years earlier, and which still hung on the opposite wall.

'Whit's that aboot the Isle of Mull?' scoffed the iconoclast across the table. 'Anither o' they Tall Tales frae the islands?'

Seeing a strong support for his arguments, the second man, to the astonishment of the locals, pressed the bell push, which had never worked in living memory. 'No, no,' said Do'l Gorm hopefully, 'You chust stamp on the floor twice like this' — and as Big Duncan put his head round the door he added: 'This chentleman would like you to take an order, Duncan. Chust make mine a small sensation and a chaser.'

There was a lull in the conversation as the drinks came through and were sampled with muttered salutations to the man standing his hand. Eyes presently gravitated to the old roadman, who appeared to have grown somewhat in stature, although it was maybe just the effects of the drink. I could see that this veritable Kai Lung among Highland raconteurs was in good form.

'Imphm!' he reflected. 'Chust another tale from the islands. Let me tell you,' he added darkly, and with contempt, 'Ther iss things in the islands here that you Sassunachs know nothing about. Up here for a few days and you think you can go home and write a book about it!' He paused to direct a jet of tobacco juice from behind his hand into the exact centre of the adjacent cuspidor. 'I am telling you the Loch Ness monster is chust a bit of string compared with some of the things I haf seen maself.

'I wass telling not long ago about the time we wass mending a pier out on the Long Island. I clean forgot to speak about the eels. Do you know, there iss eels down ther in the foundations of the pier ass thick ass the pipes that come down the hillside at Fort William for the electricity. They got big and fat on the cargoes of herrings the fishing boats would be dumping when the Government told them they had caught too much. Inteet, it wass the eels moving about that made the pier unsafe. But ther's far bigger than that.

'One morning I wass standing on Sron Crup above the lighthouse when I saw a commotion on the sea coming away up from Salen. When it came near enough I saw it wass a great eel swimming north with its head and back going up and down in the water. It would be about ten in the morning when its head came level with me — and mind you, it wass going fast — but it took 'till the afternoon before the tail came up and it disappeared away out to Coll — and, mind you, I wass watching it the whole time.'

Quick to sense the reaction of his audience, Do'l Gorm hastily held up an arresting hand indicating there was more to follow, took a delicate sip from his glass and a gulp from the tankard, and gave tongue again with a convincing delivery that effectively silenced his would-be critics.

'Of coorse', he admitted loftily, 'Ther's only my word for what I wass telling you. But ther wass the chiant eel of Loch na Beiste that the old people, yess, maybe some of them are here tonight, will be remembering. Stop you and I'll tell you about it.'

As a small crowd gathered round, I was struck by Do'l Gorm's similarity to the Ancient Mariner: *"He holds him with his glittering eye....."*

'First of aal,' he began, 'You must understand that eels iss a mystery. Ther wass some French professor I wass hearing about that said they come from some water that iss hot and full of tangles away over in America and follow some Golf Team over here to run up our rivers: but I am not believing him — I think he will be choking. Anybody in Mull will tell you eels grow from hairs that fall into the water. Let me tell you what I would do when I wass a boy. I would pull a long black hair from the tail of a horse and put it under a flat stone in the burn. A few days later, when I would turn over the stone carefully, sure anough there wass a real live eel chust where I put it.

'Now, this burn that ran past our house wass the best at growing eels in the island, because, you see, it came down from Loch na Beiste — what you would caal the Loch of the Monster. That loch wass chust hotching with eels. The water wass so good for them that a bit of sheep's wool falling in would turn into a nest of eels by the next morning.

'In this loch ther wass some old stones out in the shallows, something to do with the Little People and the old days — ach, I didn't want to know about it, for it iss no' canny to interfere. Well, the Laird brought in a gang of men to draw a plan of these stones, and they wass using a boat and a long wire rope. Seeing they wass strangers and knew nothing, they left the rope aal night in the water at the edge of the bank the first day. Next morning, when they came back, ther wass no sign of the rope, no, not a trace. But after a wee while, one of the men gave a shout, pointed to the middle of the loch and began to run. Out ther they saw the head and neck of a great thin long eel sticking up looking at them, and at once it came tearing in at them making a wash like the *Lochinvar*. The men aal let out a skreich and didn't stop running till they reached the edge of the pier three miles away, and they wouldn't move from ther until the afternoon boat for the south wass coming in, and they wass chumping for safety to her dake before the gangway was out.

'Well, after that nobody would dare to go near the loch with that eel on the watch. Ther used to be good grazing round the banks, but when the cows aal started to disappear, the loch had to be fenced off, and since the fencers refused to go near the loch a good bit of good ground wass lost. Man, the Laird wass vexed, but what could he do? Aal sorts of stories got around. The eel became a kind of roving *Each Uisge* according to the tales, and nobody would leave the house after dark: although, mind you, I believe the beast got the blame for a lot she didn't do, like the six young ewes that wass lifted from Calum Ban's croft. Well, if the eel took them she would haf to do four miles over dry ground, and I am thinking that iss chust not possible.

'After a year or two the Laird got tired of it aal and made up his mind to drain the loch, which would get rid of the beast and give him back his good land and a bit more, and let him haff a close look at the queer old stones out in the loch. It wass very shallow, except for the corner at the east wher ther wass a kind of cluff that kept the water back. So he got another gang of men from somewhere far away to set dy-namite under the cluff. Ther wass a squad of the local territorials with rifles and a big dram aal round to keep up ther courage and the eel down. But to make sure, they let loose a couple of done old cows at the far end to keep the eel busy.

'Chust ass the men lit the fuses and made for shelter, along came the eel with its head above the water and its teeth snapping and the two big lumps like the Loch Ness Monster — but these lumps wass the poor old cows. Right under the cluff the beast came to a stop, wondering what was going on — and chust at that off went the charges and the whole cluff came down on her. What with the explosion and great lumps of rock stotting off her back, the eel wass so shocked and surprised that she went down, wriggled a bit, and chust died.

'But here's the funny thing. When the water aal drained away, what did they find but the orichanal wire rope aal tangled up wher the eel had her last struggles, and among it the remains of two cows. Ther wass a thick coating of slime and scales round the rope, but that went away in a few days leaving it ass clean and free from rust ass it wass when the men left it in the water two years before.'

Unobserved by his silent and marvelling audience, Do'l Gorm reached absently for the almost untouched glass of the most vocal of his recent critics and drained it to the dregs. Then lighting his pipe he retired behind the security of the smoke screen to resume his ecstatic contemplation of the infinite.

THE QUEER VISIT

THE QUEER VISIT
OF
CALUM A'SGIOBAIR

The short December day was drawing to a close. Out in the Bay a fleet of drifters and half a dozen big trawlers tugged at their anchors and swung slowly, buffeted even in this sheltered haven by the squalls of hail and snow roaring down from the hills.

The lights of the village shone warmly and invitingly; but none radiated more peace and goodwill than the bar windows of the Maclean Arms. The usual Saturday night crowd was inside, anticipating the delights of Hogmanay, assisted by a dozen or so fishermen from the sheltering craft, clad in their loose turtle-necked woollen gansies and white rubber boots rolled down below the knees, seemingly impervious to either heat or cold. The bar-room was hot and stuffy with a mixed aroma of spirits, stale fish and damp clothing, overlain by a thick haze of tobacco smoke. Overall was the faint tank of peat smoke, for Big Duncan, the proprietor, always kept a peat fire on the go to provide strangers with the true atmosphere of the Isles.

Ensconced in his favourite seat strategically placed within arm's length of both the fire and the bar-counter, Do'l Gorm set down his half-empty glass with care and prepared to join in the conversation.

'Christmas,' he repeated, addressing himself to a young deck hand from down Fleetwood way, 'Tach, that iss maybe a Sasunnach time for eating and enchoyment, but up here, ass efferybody knows, the New Year iss the right time for that.' He concluded a little vaguely, 'You go to Church at Christmas.'

'Do you mean the Old New Year?,' squeaked a wee old man leaning on a stick, a *bodach* with an air of such venerable permanence that he might have been one of the original opponents of the alteration to the calendar. Do'l Gorm dismissed him with a withering look and wiped his moustache with a fine gesture.

'The New Year,' he repeated firmly, 'Iss the time for men to enchoy themselves. Behind them iss the Old Year with aal its troubles past; in front iss the New Year that iss always going to be a good one, and if we tell it to our friends with a drop of *Old Mull* well, why not? In the old days it would chust be the one day's holiday we would be getting and we had to make the most of it. Now ther iss football matches and week-ends that go on for ten days at the New Year.'

Here the speaker coughed pointedly and directed a look at his empty glass which was promptly refilled at the expense of the skipper of the drifter *'Pride of Lossie'* out of Banff, who had been contemplating Do'l Gorm's easy flow of words in a state of happy hypnosis. The young Englishman who had first brought up the subject tried again.

'You've never seen a proper Christmas up 'ere, that's what's wrong with you. Why, at 'ome, the very ghosts come out at Christmas. I'll bet you've never 'eard of a New Year ghost, 'ave yer?'

Do'l Gorm did not reply at once, but stared with his faded blue eyes past his questioner, past the door of the bar-room — shaken at that moment by an extra vicious gust of wind — at some vision of his own. A pause came in the general conversation, and every eye centred on him.

'Ther may still be some of you here,' he began, 'Who will be remembering Calum a'Sgiobair that lived over ther on the island?' 'I mind him fine,' squeaked the *bodach*. 'He wass a MacNeill.' 'Why did they call him the Skipper?' someone enquired.

'Tach, because his grandfather used to run a smack between here and the islands. Besides, his mother was a MacDonald. What else would you be caaling him?'

Having thus established the question of identity, the speaker took up the thread of his story.

'Calum wass a man that liked his dram. Effery Saturday night he would row over in yon old boat of his until he got the enchine into her for the lobster fishing. It was an old enchine he lifted off a launch somebody left on the shore, and it ran on sea water, because I used to see it maself spurting out the side when he got her going.

'But the one night he would neffer miss wass Hogmanay. Rain, snow or fine, his boat would come to the steps below the pier chust about this time and he would wait until twelve o'clock to bring in the New Year. Then effery time he would say: "Well, boys, we'll be with you next New Year — that's a promise." Then he would walk down to his boat and row away back to the island. He neffer came first-footing, which wass a pity, for nobody effer saw him the worse of what he took.

'The last Hogmanay we saw him wass a bit like tonight, only worse. That wass the time the big ship went ashore and broke up on the Sgeir Dubh and kept us in boxes of fruit and carpets for weeks after. Ther wass other wrecks, too, for that wass the worst storm we effer saw. We wass aal standing here — it would be chust about now. The wind wass at its very worst. Nothing could face it, even from ass near as the island.

' "We'll no' be seeing Calum the night," we wass aal saying, when a squall burst against the windows and the door smashed back against the wall: and ther wass Calum standing in the opening. He wass looking ass happy ass if it wass a summer day and the boat full of lobsters, although the water wass dripping off him and his cap wass lashed down with a piece of string. He came over beside us.

' "I'm a bit late," he said. "It was kind of rough coming over and I had to take to the oars, because the enchine stoppped."

'He had his glass or two and talked away with us, but aal the time there wass something strange about him. The water kept dripping off his clothes and a piece of seaweed wass caught up in his pocket: not that we thought much about that, for he wass a great man for carrying round a bunch of dulse with him for chewing.

'They neffer minded much about closing time on Hogmanay then, and it wass near midnight when we came out to the pierhead to see Calum off and take in the New Year. Out in the dark the storm wassn't quite so bad, the wind easing off.

'Well, ass the clock struck twelve over at the other end of the village, a quietness came over us. Not the usual thing at aal. Nobody wass singing or shaking hands or reaching for the bottle. In the dark we could see Calum, standing up very straight and tall, like a young man, at the top of the steps. But he made no move to come over and shake hands like other years. Instead he raised his arm and spoke in the Gaelic — "Well, goodbye, boys," he said, "And many happy years to effery one of you. Blessings rest with you."

'We suddenly felt cold and a bit frightened. We came closer together, shook hands quietly and gave greetings (for it would neffer do to forget the occasion) and went straight home to our beds. It wass the first time since we wass boys that any of us remembered being in bed the first day of the year. Two days later we heard that Calum's body had been found washed up on the Camus Buie, his cap still lashed on his head with a piece of string. No trace of his boat wass effer found.

'Now, here's the thing.   Later on, when we wass talking about it, none of us could remember touching him that night, even at the crowded bar.   And although he wass dripping wet, Big Duncan's father there swore ther wass not a drop of water to be seen on the floor wher he had been standing; and the queer way he left us on the pier, without his usual mention of next Hogmanay.   Now, tell, me this: did Calum a'Sgiobair come to us before he wass drowned, or wass it afterwards, to keep his promise?'

In the dead silence which had fallen on the room no-one observed Do'l Gorm as he reached silently for the brimming tankard which was standing untouched in front of the skipper of the drifter *'Pride of Lossie',* out of Banff.

BOATS AND BOCANS

BOATS AND BOCANS

It was seldom you would hear Do'l Gorm discoursing on anything esoteric or uncanny, but on one occasion a poaching story drifted naturally into its creepy aftermath. He told me about it this day when I hurried up through the soaking bracken to shelter for a while in the contraption he had erected under the lip of the quarry. I found him comfortably smoking as he contemplated the wind-whipped waters below.

'It iss the sort of day I will soon be going home to change my wet clothes,' he greeted me. 'I'll be with you down the road!'

'But you aren't wet yet,' I returned, eyeing him over.

'No, no,' agreed the roadman complacently, 'But I will be before I get home.

'It iss reminding me of a storm Lachie and me got caught in one time out in the middle of the Sound a while ago. Before the rheumatics came on him so badly. I'll tell you about it before we go, but don't let on to anybody.

'The two of us used to go fishing quite a bit in the boat we used to keep round at the Port-a'Choit. Many's the time we spent fishing over the bank beyond the lighthouse and round the Stirks rocks. Man, yon's the place! Ther iss lythe and piocach ass long ass my arm in shoals above the beds of tangles. I haf seen us, one at the oars, and the other sitting on a plank across the stern end with four bamboo rods out, two white flies on each rod and a fish on effery fly. You needed to haf four hands. It was nothing to come home with two or three hundred fish. Some of them wass so big you couldn't pull them in without breaking something, so what we did wass to drop the rod overboard and leave it floating to play the fish out, and when we pulled round again, we chust had to pull in the fish.

'I mind once ther wass some towerists staying at the Maclean Arms who hired a boat for an evening's fishing. Of coorse they were knowing what to do better than the boatman — it wss Calum a 'Sgiobair, and he wass telling me about it himself. Well, one of them hooked a big lythe. He couldn't get it in, so he chust dropped the rod overboard. "That's what they told us to do in the Hotel," the man said when Calum tried to stop him. "Ach, well, maybe," said Calum, as he looked over the side where the rod was sinking far down into the tangles. "But you neffer told them you wass going to use your greenheart salmon rod!"

'But I wass going to tell you about Lachie and me. Well, if the tide wass right we might leave the Stirks and slip over to Camusbuie on the other side. Ther iss a burn comes down ther between the sand and the rocks making a sheltered wee inlet chust perfect for a splash net. Of coorse, it gave us a long row, but it wass worth it and dead quiet; chust the bogs and the cliffs ashore and nobody within miles to see us lifting a few seatrout.

'This time I am telling you about we landed over at Camusbuie in the late evening with the tide well in and no more than a swell on the water and very little wind. We put out the net very careful; then Lachie went up to the head of the pool and began to heave in big stones to drive the fish back down, wher, of coorse, they would run into the net we had stretched across. I had my hand on the rope, and I wass feeling by the chugs that ther wass something doing; and right enough, when we pulled it in, there wass a dozen seatrout in it up to four pounds.

'Now, aal the time we wass so busy we wassn't thinking about the weather outside. We found the sky wass filling up and coming down and the wind and waves getting up, and, mind you, I'm sure it would be six miles of a row home. So we pushed the net and the fish anyway into a sack, threw it into the boat and pushed off in a hurry. We wass feeling pretty fresh, so at first we got on fine.

'But chust when we wass halfway across the wind backed into the east and began to blow a gale. It wass very dark, and the boat began leaping and chumping, for we wass pulling half into the wind. We began to row, yess, for our very lives, with the spray beginning to come over us in sheets and the big waves spouting round us like depth charges. Although we wass good at the oars we wass getting near bate, and for aal we could do, I could see from the way the lighthouse was moving that we wass drifting fast to the open sea. Then I called out to Lachie that our only chance to stay afloat wass to tie the sack and spare oars to the painter and let it out for a sea anchor to keep her head to the waves — and trust to luck.

'Chust at that the wind dropped for a wee while to gather itself for what I knew would be our finish. We pulled in the sea anchor and put our backs to the oars again, this time taking the shortest road across to the island that would land us at Ploody Bay. A good chob we did, for ther wass only fifty yards to spare between us and the last point of shelter when the storm really broke on us. Well, at least we wass in the shelter with the high cliffs of Ploody Bay aal round us and the bare black rocks at the foot of them. Even by daylight we couldn't haf climbed the cliffs, let alone in the dark. But at least we wass safe, unless the wind changed.

'After a while, when we wass feeling better, "Lachie,"I said, "Do you mind yon wee cave chust along the shore from us. Do you think we should make for it? We'll be out of the rain and wind anyway."

' "Yess, we can make it easy enough," said Lachie, but a bit doubtfully. "But are you forgetting that iss the cave they caal *Uamh nam Bocan*, that nobody effer went near?".

' "*Bocan* or no *bocan*," says I, "We'll see if we can tie up ther and see if we can get some shelter." '

(At this point I should explain that the Gaelic word *Bocan* — pronounced 'Boch-Kan' — means a ghost.)

'We rowed along in the dark listening to the howling of the wind and the spouting of the waves off the point until we came to the black entrance to the cave. Not very wide and a hard scramble to reach it after we tied up the boat secure at bow and stern. It wass chust a wee short cave and quite dry at the far end. You could neffer reach it from the land, only by boat. We sat down at the dry end, ate what wass left of our food and washed it down with the wee dram we had still left — and, my chove, we needed it. We had a smock, too, and began to feel a bit better, so we stretched out the best way we could to wait for the morning. Lachie kept grumbling away about something sharp that wass pushing into his back. But ther wass more than sharp stones that wass keeping us on edge, for we chust coudn't get warm, and it wassn't because of our damp clothes. I began thinking about stories I had heard about this cave that nobody wass effer inside, and I'm sure Lachie wass thinking the same, for he kept twisting and turning. I can toll you I wished I wass safe at home in my own bed.

'When I did fall into a kind of a sleep it wass to dream of the old galleys they used to haf: ther wass a shouting in my ears not of the wind and the waves. Of coorse, you will know that Ploody Bay got its name after a terrible fight, the biggest that effer took place between fleets of galleys in the islands, between the Lord of the Isles and his nephew Angus, a fighting MacDonald. Old folk say anybody could choin in, for the Macleans wass in it too. Anyway, the sea wass red with blood, so many had been killed: and that is how the Bay got its name.

'In the morning, when we came right awake, it wass with the sun shining in our faces round the high point, and the wind and storm clean gone. I looked round at Lachie, for he had given a chump back on to his knees, staring down with his mouth open. My own heart nearly stopped beating when I looked. Lying ther under us wass the remains of three or four men, the skulls and big bones and a few scraps of leather and cloth. The sharp thing Lachie had been complaining about wass all that wass left of a rusted claymore. Maybe it wass wounded men that crawled ashore and found ther way in to die after the battle.

'We both let out a *sgiamh* of fright that startled nearly effery scart in the Bay, and gave one leap over the rocks into the boat. I mind the way we fought with the ropes to cast off and when we got at the oars — if we had rowed like that last night we would haf gone through the storm like a submarine. Once we were round the Lighhouse Point we felt safe again, although shaken up with the fright. Still we had sense enough to put the bag overboard with the net and the fish and a weight to keep it down, with a floating marker to let us pick it up later.

'My chove, Calamore wass glad to see us safely home at the pier, for they had given us up for lost. We said we had been lucky in getting into a sheltered cove round the point. We would neffer tell anybody about our night in the *Uamh nam Bocan*. They would chust haf laughed and said it wass chust another story — or else we had been at the bottle. They did wonder sometimes why we would neffer go fishing far into Ploody Bay. But no; Lachie and maself chust know ther iss some things in this world, or maybe out of it, that iss not to be spoken about.'

BRIDES AND BEES

DO'L GORM
ON
BRIDES AND BEES

One hot afternoon in summer, as I was approaching Do'l Gorm's house, I became aware of a thin humming from the other side of the garden dyke. Suddenly the gate burst open and out shot the man himself, full of obscure Gaelic imprecations, slapping and tearing at his head that was swathed around like that of a veiled Toureg. I gathered that his bees had swarmed and that one or more had penetrated the layers of old curtains he wore to protect his face from his vicious attackers. You see, although his arms were so scarred and leathery with years of stone-chapping that bees, midges, clegs and all the rest simply blunted their stings on them, he was most sensitive about his face. In my long acquaintance with him, a bee was the only thing I ever saw that called forth his latent powers of acceleration. I approached with caution, ensuring first that he had lost his nimbus of irate insects.

'These old curtains is no use any more,' he lamented, fingering a rapidly swelling prominence above his right eye. 'Come away in and we'll haf a cup of tea and I'll be putting the blue bag on this sting.'

Presently we were sitting over biscuits and cups of black tea. 'Whatever possessed you to keep bees,' I enquired, 'When they give you so much trouble? I'm sure if you had a wife she'd soon make you clear them out. Anyway,' I challenged him, 'A fine man like yourself should have been married long since, you with your wee house and all these jobs at your finger ends.'

Do'l Gorm looked evasively coy and rubbed his head with an air of embarrassment, until absent-mindedly touching the inflamed area he winced and grunted: 'Tach, no fear! I haf more sense. Man, even with maself, and the dog and the bees and the cat it iss a bad enough place for gossip. What would it be like with a woman ass well? Although, mind you, they come in handy sometimes.

'You mind the three brothers MacDougall that lived in the Port-a' Choit Road aal by themselves? Well, the two older ones wass always getting on to Peter, the younger one. If ther wass a dirty chob to do, it wass for Peter — "Away you and fetch the stirks — bring in the sack of meal — go out and fill the peat basket — the cows are needing milking....." It wass Peter this and Peter that, but he chust did it and said nothing. It wass one winter day when they aal came home wet and cold to their empty house and the fire to light that the older brothers had this idea.

' "Peter," they said, "We are needing a woman in the house. Chust you be looking out for a wife." But Peter wassn't a bit put out. After they got settled he put on his collar and tie and his other boots and out he walked. But wait you: he knew fine what he wass doing. For ten years he had had his eyes on a widow woman, a right cheerful sort she wass, with her own house and a nice wee shop that would suit Peter chust fine. Well, when he put up the idea she chumped at the chance, for Peter wass in his prime then, a fresh man of only sixty. Man, the two other brothers wass so mad they would hardly go to the wedding.'

'Yes, Donald,' I broke in. 'That's all very well, but what about yourself? Why didn't you get married?'

'Well,' replied the other with some satisfaction, 'Chust between you and me ther wass one woman I had a chob to shake off. She used to live next door, Anna Gorach, they caaled her, but that wass a while after her father died. Mind you, he wass always thin and hungry-looking. She wass always at the gate or the fence when I would be coming home. "Oh, Donald," she would caal, "Would you like a taste of my scones?" — or maybe it would be a lump of pudding or pancakes — chust wee things like that. Well, I would haf to take them for politeness. But if you dropped a scone it would crack the cement or else make a splash of dough. Neffer twice the same. No wonder her father died. Even when I offered the things to the dog he would slide away under the chair and I had to give him a wee kick before he would nibble at them. Although I could see fine she wass doing her best she neffer even by acident got it right.

'After a few years of this she began to drop hints about how time wass slow to pass for lonely peple, and what a good price my house would fetch; so I began to think she wass maybe making up to me. It wass a while later she began to imachine things. She would go through the streets taaking to people that wassn't ther. Man, it was sad. That wass when people began to caal her Anna Gorach.

'I got no more scones or puddings that stotted or splashed. Instead of handing things across the fence she would caal them, until she would get that excited I would haf to stay inside or come home late when she wass settled down in the house. My cat wass chust tormented with her, and she would shout over at me —"Yess, you ther, the spite of you, even teaching your cat to chump on the roof and pull off the slates!"

'But neffer you mind. I got the idea one day after I saw her hitting the air with a towel and tearing into the house with some sort of bee or wasp after her. "Man," I said to myself, "The ferry thing. I'll get some bees." So I got a swarm from the gardener over at Achahonish and put it in a box over against her fence.

'But I don't know what iss worse, a bee's sting or a woman's tongue, for she would still caal things through the upstairs window — and the bees turned out to be ass vicious a bunch ass effer came out of a hive. So maybe I wass no better off. Of coorse, I got a little honey after a while, when I got to know how to manage them and wait until they wass quite tired out, but I neffer went near without something round my face.

'Vicious! You haffn't an idea. They say that when bees iss swarming they are that happy they will sit on your shoulder and let you lift them by the handful chust humming with delight. Not my bees, though! When they swarmed, it isn't to swarm but to go looking for trouble! Ther wass the time of the manse garden party to raise money for the mending of the steeple. The afternoon turned out fine and hot after the rain and effery body wass well pleased. My bees was in fine trim, too, and chust ready for mischief after being kept in for days with the rain.

'By good luck the people had spent nearly aal their money by the time the Member of Parliament began to speak. He wass staying at the Big House at the time. Well, the people wass chust finishing their teas in the big tent and gathering round to listen when my bees swarmed — and they made a bee-line for the Member of Parliament. When I saw what wass going to happen I put a piece in my pocket and went up to fish the lochs for the rest of the day, because I knew the keeper wass at the party with the chentry.

'But Lachie wass telling me aal about it later on. They say you neffer saw a place empty so quickly. It was effery one for herself. If a tent stood in the way they chust went through it and out at the other side. The minister himself wass using words that brought more people to his Kirk afterwards than effer before, out of respect and admiration.

'Of coorse, they blamed my bees; but, well, as I wassn't ther and didn't know anything about it, and when I came home the bees wass aal quiet and happy in their box, full of sugar and cham from the garden party, nobody could say a word.

'And Anna Gorach? Poor woman, I wass sorry for her. They had to come and take her away to Lochgilphead, she got so bad. But they said she wass quite happy so long ass you give her a pan of flour and a chug of water.

'No,' he concluded, puffing out an ominous mushroom cloud, 'No wife for me! Weemen won't leave a man in peace to enchoy his own wee comforts in his own way without nagging aal the pleasure out of it.'

THE BONGA

One day The Bonga was listening with impatience to a man from the village who was boasting — not without reason — of the huge lythe and mackerel to be caught out in the Sound of Mull round the reefs they call The Stirks.

'Ach, that's nothing,' broke in The Bonga contemptuously. 'Last week I am catching flounders in the Sound of Iona that thick you couldn't see their kidneys for fat!'

Later they were discussing the Flood of the Old Testament.

'The first bird Noah sent out was a pigeon,' remarked the other man, 'And it came back to the Ark. The second he sent was a raven, and it neffer came back. Why would that be?'

The Bonga thought for a long time. 'Ach, well,' he concluded gravely and sagely, 'Maybe it would be finding a braxie sheep.' (That is, a sheep that has died of natural causes, often an item of food for the crofters.)

TALES TOLD ROUND

THE FIRESIDE

THE STRONG MAN

THE STRONG MAN

One day when the Strong Man was walking along he came across a neighbour whose cart had slipped off the road and was keeled over with one wheel deeply sunk in the ditch and the poor horse lying between the shafts exhausted by its efforts to dislodge it. Sizing up the situation, the Strong Man took off his jacket and handed it to the other man. Then he went down, unyoked the horse, raised it to its feet and pulled it back up to the road. Then going down to the cart he gripped the shafts and began to heave until the wheel eased out of the mud; then with a great effort he tore the whole cart free and dragged it back on to the road. As he resumed his jacket, he remarked to his grateful neighbour: 'Indeed, I am not surprised the poor horse was done. I had a big enough job to move the cart myself!'

(The author was assured of the veracity of the story by a lady who used to live not far from the Strong Man's house.)

THE COLL MAN

A man from the island of Coll was staying with friends in London. One evening they went out for dinner, and at the table the visitor was fascinated by a very attractive girl sitting on the opposite side of the table. Turning to the man beside him, he enquired: 'I wonder who iss that fine looking girl across the table from us?'. 'Oh', said his amused neighbour, 'That's just a Call Girl.' 'Well, well,' said the islander thoughtfully, 'Chust fancy that. Me in Coll aal my life and I never met her!'

THE SPONGER

THE SPONGER

The meanest man I ever met was Archie Ruadh, who, although he seemed to live on nothing but the Pension, was often enough in the Bank, although he took good care nobody was at the counter at the time. If Archie couldn't cadge a drink he could make a glass of lemonade with a dash of beer last for a whole night. However, he was "No' so far back", as we say of someone unexpectedly smart.

You probably don't remember the black bottles we used to have for whisky, which, in those civilised days, you could get filled up from a keg at the grocer's quite cheaply. They would hold perhaps a sixth of a gallon. Well, we discovered that Archie Ruadh had hit on a novel idea. What he would do was to push a piece of sponge into an empty black bottle until the space was half filled with it. Then he would go to Betsy the Grocer's shop and ask for a small order — tea, sugar, a pat of butter, oh yes, and would she just give him a fill of the bottle. When Betsy added it all up, it came to — say eighteen shillings. Archie would upend his purse on the counter and shake it (we used to say the moths didn't come out — they were all dead!) and bemoan: 'Oh, Betsy, I've only got twelve shilllings. You'll just have to pour the whisky back into the keg,' which was duly done by the unsuspecting Betsy.

When he arrived home he would upend the 'empty' bottle and squeeze the sponge with a thin porridge spurtle over a cup and collect perhaps two glasses of whisky!

NATURAL POLITENESS

NATURAL POLITENESS

There is one village in our island with a population whose natural inquisitiveness is well disguised by a veneer of ostensible indifference.   A stranger walking along sees in front of him an empty street betwen two rows of houses with the windows heavily curtained; but the minute he is past the place buzzes like a beehive.   Curtains twitch, faces peer out after him and doors open as the *Caileachs* hurry out to discuss everything from his walk to his possible bank balance.   He has made their day.

This was well known to a local laird who used to go about on horseback — a resourceful man with a sense of humour, who decided to catch them out.   So one day, when the distinctive clip-clop of his horse's hooves was heard coming along the street, the women indoors all came to the alert with eager anticipation and their usual timing.   This time, however, when they came hurrying into the street after he had passed, they found to their chagrin and embarrassment that he had mounted the horse facing its tail, and was doffing his hat and calling greetings to them as they emerged unsuspecting.

THE SORE KNEE

Old Do'l Ruadh, limping a bit with the rheumatism, met the doctor one day as he was hirpling up the Back Brae.

'And how are you today?' enquired the doctor conversationally.

'Och, it iss my knee,' replied Do'l Ruadh, bending down to rub the offending limb.

'Eh, eh,' replied the doctor, 'You must remember it is getting older all the time'

'Yess, yess,but it iss the same age ass my other knee, and that one iss fine!'

DAL na SCATTAN

DAL NA SCATTAN

Over at Acharonich you will come to a field with the strange name of *'Dal na Scattan'* — the Field of Herrings. It was so named after a freak rainstorm had left it covered with tiny fish, probably the result of a minor water spout on adjacent Loch Tuath that carried up into the air surface water containing a shoal of young fish.

DEEP SEA FROGS

During one of the salvage operations in the 'twenties on the sunken Armada galleon in Tobermory Bay, the local headmaster, highly respected and a keen naturalist, was employed during the school holidays supervising the screens over which passed the stream of mud, water, debris, and (hopefully) doubloons brought up from the timbers of the wreck by powerful pumps. One of the deck hands, a former pupil, decided to play a trick on him, so one day he slipped a pocketful of frogs he had brought out from the shore into the gushing outflow.

These were spotted at once by the excited headmaster. The outcome was a report to the Press on the existence of frogs on the bottom of Tobermory Bay, raising an animated correspondence that went on for weeks.

The same publicity failed to accompany the appearance of an old alarm clock which appeared in the same place soon after. The idea of a modern timepiece appearing among the elusive doubloons was just too much for the imagination!

EMERGENCY

126

THE EMERGENCY

Many years ago Malcolm MacDonald took over the tenancy of the island of Inch Kenneth. This was long before the days of motor boats, and the short ferry across from Gribun could be rough enough at times for a rowing boat. It was arranged with the folk at Gribun that if Malcolm was faced with a real emergency he would light the big bonfire he kept ready at the slipway and the Gribun men would row over to bring help.

One very wild day the bonfire began to smoke and blaze with its signal of urgency. Over in Gribun four of the crofters launched a boat from the beach and toiled at the oars amid showers of spray and high waves, until soaked to the skin they drew in with relief at the jetty on Inch Kenneth. To their surprise, there was Malcolm jumping up and down with impatience.

'Boys, boys,' he shouted, 'Did you bring any tobacco with you? I'm clean out of it!'

LIMPID CLARITY

A minister had in his charge two kirks situated at the opposite ends of a long loch. One day there appeared on the door of the one of the kirks a notice which read:
'There will be no service here next Sunday as the minister will be preaching at the bottom of the Loch.'

THE CROIG SMACK

The owner of a smack sailing out of Croig was engaged to carry a cargo of potatoes to Greenock. Knowing no English, he was worried about how to speak to the Sasunnachs down there, especially as he would probably be landing there about New Year's Day, so he asked the advice of a friend.

'When you reach Greenock,' he was told, 'You will first meet the piermaster. He will say to you "Where are you from?" and "What is your cargo?" and then "A happy New Year." All you will need to say is "Croig" and "Potatoes", and then "The same to you," all of which the owner of the smack memorised.

When he came alongside the pier at Greenock, right enough the piermaster came up, and the following conversation took place:
'What is your cargo?' 'Croig,' said the smack owner.
'Where are you from?' "Potatoes."
'I think you are a fool!' 'The same to you!'

THE MESSAGE BOY

Exasperated island grocer to lazy message boy:-
'You're here yet and you're no' back! Did you no' get the message? The next time I am sending a fool I will go maself!'

GLENGORM

Did you ever hear how the name 'Glengorm' originated? Up to the middle of the 19th century, the district was known as Sorne, but just about then the estate changed hands and a new Laird took over whose name came to be hated. This was James Forsyth, the man responsible for drastic clearances on his estate, including certain mean and unscrupulous legal dealings with his tenants in Dervaig village. You will read all about it in the findings of the Public Enquiry held in the '80s.

Having cleared five crofters from a stretch of good land he laid down policies and gardens, in the middle of which he built a handsome mansion house. As time went on he began to think of an appropriate name for the building. His first choice of 'Dunara' was dropped, for this old fort, after which he sought to name the house, lies several miles away. Then he asked the advice of an old woman living in one of the few houses he had spared.

'Call your fine new house "Glengorm"' she suggested; and when he asked the meaning of the word she explained it meant the 'Blue Glen'. The delight expressed by the laird with this lovely name would have been shortlived if he had suspected that the cynical old woman was commemorating for all time the days when the glen was indeed blue — with the smoke from the townships he had burned.

The laird never slept a night in Glengorm Castle. A few days before he was to move in, a bat flew out into his face as he opened the door, an omen of disaster, as everyone said. Sure enough, he took ill and died a few days later.

TALES TOLD BY
CALUM NAN CROIG

CALUM NAN CROIG — HIMSELF

Calum nan Croig was no legendary figure, but a very gifted story-teller who hailed from Croig, the little inlet a mile or two from our village, with its tiny jetty, old inn (now a private house), and a few scattered houses. In him, the highly developed art of convincing exaggeration mesmerised his listeners. Of course, his stories were in the Gaelic tongue, and in translating them into the poor medium of the English, much is lost of the original asides and nuances.

For instance, according to himself, he was an expert at the tying of trout flies: '.....for the fishing, you know. Ther wass one night I wass sitting at the kitchen table tying flies with the lamp for the seatrout. A strange thing happened. Every time I finished making a fly and put it down beside me — the next time I looked it wass gone. Aal right. I tied another one, put it down, sat back and lit my pipe, keeping an eye on the fly. Do you know, I wass tying them that good the spiders wass coming down from the kitchen ceiling to carry them away.'

There was only one occasion I heard of Calum being put off his stride. This was when a young nephew of his working in John Brown's shipyard in Glasgow was staying with him at the Glasgow Fair.

Calum was very partial to cabbages and was describing a particularly fine one he had grown in the garden the year before.

'It wass that big that when I made the first cut in it, I found a nest in the middle with a hen and twelve chickens.   Although my wife kept using a bit of that cabbage every day, it lasted the whole winter and into the Spring.'

His nephew thought over this for a while, and then remarked: 'You are reminding me of the big biler we wis working on in the yaird jist before ah left.   It wis that big that when ah threw ma hammer intae it at the end of the day it took a minute tae reach the bottom.'

'Man, that would be a big boiler,' conceded Calum without suspicion.   'Now, I wonder what it would be for?'

'Ach, it was fur tae bile yer big cabbage in,' replied his nephew, edging strategically for the door.

THE NORTH POLE

Peigi Chalum lived all by herself in a dilapidated cottage a mile or so along the main road.   Instead of shoes she went about with her feet wrapped in sacking.   Thanks to the Pension she was able to remain independent, although she was regarded as peculiar. Probably she was just desperately lonely, for she would haunt the road-end at her house and stop passersby to give them some message to collect from the village, however trivial, just to speak to someone.   She always managed to be there when they returned, so on-one was inconvenienced.

She was greedy for news — anything.   One day when an acquaintance told her that an explorer had discovered the North Pole, the news was received by her as a real tit-bit.   After thinking it over for a long time, her eyes shining with excitement, she remarked: 'Indeed!   Well, well!   He'll be all right for firewood now!'

THE PONY

That brings me to a typical Calum nan Croig story.

'I wass assistant keeper over at the Benmore estate,' he began. 'Oh, a great hill for stags. Not one under twelve points, and two ponies for bringing down the beasts after the chentlemen had been on a stalk. One of the ponies wass old, well past her best, but she wass that willing nobody had the heart to put her away.

'This day I wass coming down in a thick mist with a fine big stag on the back of the pony. It wass one of these mists so thick that when the dog ran over the edge of the cliff it came down as chently ass if it had a para-chute on — like falling in the water. Anyway, chust among yon rocks by the burn, the poor pony slupped and came down heavy between two rocks, and when I tried to lift her I wass vexed to find she had broken her back and couldn't move. I could do nothing for her then, so I took the stag off her, put it on my own back and went away down the hill to the house.

'I kept thinking of the look in the poor pony's eyes when I had to leave her; so after tea I went out, cut a straight branch from a rowan tree at the gate, got out a lot of ropes and bandages, and went away up the hill, for the mist had cleared away. Yess, ther she wass lying chust wher I had left her. So I straightened her up, put the branch along her back and lashed it tight for a splint with the ropes and bandages. After that I got her on her feet and chently led her to yon grassy place beside the burn and left her ther wher she would be safe.

'It wass ten days before I could get up the hill again to see her, and what do you think I found? Ther she wass ass fat and frisky ass ever — with a fine young rowan tree growing out of her back!'

THE BIG SHIP

THE BIG SHIP

The fact that the maritime experiences of Calum nan Croig were confined to the lobster boat he kept moored in the inlet near his house detracted nothing from his story of the Big Ship.

'One day,' he announced, 'I wass called out urchently to take command of a great sailing ship, for her captain had died very sudden chust when they were setting sail on a voyage round the world.

'She wass that big it took me half the day to climb the ladder to her dake. When I got ther I told the crew to weigh the anchors and set the sails. They told me ther wass a fine garden laid out away up at the crow's nest, so although it wass a long way I climbed up the rigging to see for maself. Yess, ther wass a big garden with some fine crops, especially cabbages, and a small field of oats and turnips. I am sure they wass growing that well because the crew could get any amount of seaweed for manure. At first I wass a bit worried about how the crew could gather in the crops and manage the ship as well; but the wind kept fair and they wass able to do the two jobs just fine.

'Ther wass one thing that kept us back. When we wass off the Mull of Kintyre I put my hand in my pocket for my pipe, and I wass that vexed to find that I had left it on the stern of the boat at Croig. So I gave orders to turn the ship and go back for it. Do you know, the spars wass that wide that they swept half the sheep off the Mull of Kintyre when we went about.

'The mate told me they had to grow the crops to feed the 300 cows in the byres down below, but mind you, although they had aal those cows on board, they did not have a single bull. However, when the crew wass fishing over the side they hauled up four seals. One of them wass a bull seal, so they took it below to serve the cows: but the strange thing was that aal the calves turned out to be seals. They had to let them go, and that is why you will see aal those colonies of seals along the west coast.

'We sailed on and on across the oceans. In one place the moon wass that big and close that the masts cut out a big slice in the passing. You will see the mark to this day. We traded in aal kinds of places, with brown men and black men and yellow men. It wass chust when we had a full cargo and turned for home that a strange sickness fell on the ship and the crew began to die one after another. I can tell you I had a busy time of it, what with slipping the dead men over the side, looking after the sick ones, milking the cows, minding the sails and sailing the ship, for soon I wass the only living soul on board.

'Then one morning when I came on dake I saw a strange man standing ther dressed like an atmiral, with gold braid and medals aal over him.

' "And who might you be?" I asked him, "And what are you doing on my ship?"

' "Aha," he says, "I am Sahtan himself, and I haf come to fetch you the way I did the rest of the crew." — and aal the time he had to keep moving his feet in the dake or the tar would haf melted under them with the heat.

' "You're a liar," I shouted back at him. "You will have to prove it to me who you are."

' "Aal right," roared Sahtan back at me, "We'll soon see to that. We'll set each other tasks to do; if you fail, you belong to me: if I fail, or the ship gets her anchor down before we are decided, you will go free."

'We drew for the first test, and I wass lucky. It wass Sahtan to start. So thinking to drown him in the heavy seas, I says to Sahtan — "Away you go out on the bowsprit and stay ther for one hour." — but it wass no use: the waves chust turned to steam when they touched him.

'Next day it wass Sahtan's turn. "Away you go up the main mast," he orders, "And drive a nine-inch nail into the top of the mast with your bare fist."

'Up I go, and I haf only half an inch of the nail still to go in when Sahtan is shouting up at me real urgent — "*Stad! Stad!,* or you will be driving the mast down through the keel of the ship!"

'That night I got ready for Sahtan's second test. I went down to the chain locker wher the anchor chain was stored — ther wass three miles of it on the Big Ship. I carried barrels of grease from the hold and covered the whole chain from end to end. I had chust come on dake when I felt sure I could smell the peat smoke of home, and yess, over our bows I saw the wild headland of Caliach, with the peat smoke blowing out to sea from the crofts ashore.

' "Now, Sahtan," I shouts, and Sahtan stands before me. "You are beat, for here we are home again. Your second task iss to pull back the anchor chain." When I knocked out the wedges the big anchor began to pull the chain out. Sahtan, in a rage, let out a screech at losing and grabs the anchor chain to pull it back in. But it wass no use. The greasy chain slipped through his grip, and the anchor went down until it reached the bottom. With that, ther wass a great flash, a puff of smock, and Sahtan was gone, leaving me the winner safely back home.

'And that iss the story of the first voyage I made round the world on the Big Ship.'

THE OPERATION

Well versed in the medical traditions of the island (whose practitioners, the Beaton doctors, were famous throughout the Hebrides from the days of St. Columba to the early eighteenth century), Calum nan Croig was naturally a profound admirer of the local doctor.

This day, Calum had been persuaded to act as boatman on Loch Frisa for three eminent surgeons up from London for a holiday. Loch Frisa, as everyone knows, is that long, narrow loch stocked with a fighting strain of beautifully spotted red-fleshed trout. As the day wore on, Calum became increasingly bored by the three anglers, whose volume of shop talk was in the inverse ratio to their ability to catch fish. He gathered that but for miraculous operations performed by the talented speakers, half the population of London would have finished up inevitably in the cemetary. At length they decided to row in and enjoy their packed lunches on the warm shingly beach below the plantation halfway along the loch. But still the talk went on, one waiting with impatience to cap the other's story, just like golfers at the nineteenth hole.

After a time, when Calum had champed down his thick sandwiches and shared appreciatively in a dram (for they were decent enough fellows after all), he lit his pipe and gave tongue in one of the small silences.

'You know, chentlemean,' he interjected, 'Your talk of aal these operations iss reminding me of a very clever doctor we haf here in Mull — Doctor Mackinnon: I'm sure you will be knowing him.'

The surgeons indicated a polite disclaimer.

'Yess,' continued Calum with the imperturbability of a tank going through a cornfield, 'Ther wass one operation he did: oh, it would be nothing like the ones you would be doing in London. Maybe I could be telling you about it.

'It wass the time the shepherd away at the head of Glen Cannel took bad. They managed to get word to the doctor and he set off with his black bag ass far ass the road would take him. Ther wass three more miles of road he had to walk before he came to the shepherd's cottage, wher the wife wass waiting for him at the door, very anxious and crying away into her apron. In he went at once to the bedroom, wher the shepherd wass moaning and groaning on the bed. After a while he came out looking very serious.

' "Yess, inteet," he says, "The man iss very ill. His stomach iss clean gone and we chust dare not move him. Ther iss only the one chance we haf to save him: to give him a new stomach. Do you haf anything about the house that would do?"

'The wife, crying away like anything, said "Och, doctor, I chust do not know. Well, ther iss maybe the wee calf in the shed....." — "No", says the doctor, "Far too big." "Well," she thinks again, "Ther iss the cat....." "No, no; far too wee." "Ther iss nothing else," she wept, "Except the pet lamb." — "The very thing!" cries the doctor.

'So he gets out his knives and bottles and things, and puts the shepherd on the kitchen table and the lamb on the dresser. In no time at aal he has taken out the lamb's stomach and fixed it inside the shepherd; man, a fine chob he made of it: I saw the stitching for maself later on. "Now," says the doctor to the wife, "Chust you keep him in the house for a week or two before you let him back on the hill." '

Calum nan Croig halted and prepared to light another nauseous handful of black tobacco in his pipe.

'Well, man, well?' enquired the surgeons, who had sat up and taken notice as the tale developed. 'Surely an operation like that could not possibly have been a success. Did the man die?'

'Not a success?' repeated Calum in astonishment, peering over the match suspended over the bowl of his pipe: 'Did he die? Of coorse it wass a success. He wass a better man than effer before, except he would keep nip-nipping away at the grass. In fact, he lambed the next year!'

NOTHING IN IT!

In the corner of a field not far from one of the little piers in the island, you would see, up to some years ago, a stack of drainage tiles, overgrown, broken,and forgotten among the long grass. Many years ago the tenant of the place decided to order a few tiles to drain a corner of the field. Now, neither the man nor his son was very clever, certainly when it came to figuring. However, the son stepped out the distances and decided they would need 100 tiles to do the job; so he sat down and began to compose a letter to the suppliers. When he had finished, his father, who had been looking over his shoulder, remarked cautiously: 'Now, you had better be adding another wee "0" to your figures in case we are a bit short, and the makers will know to send plenty.' And so the order was sent away. In due course a cargo of 1000 tiles was delivered, and the unwanted surplus was left forlornly.

By the way, talking about tiles, did you ever hear of the man who, in the early days of sanitation, proudly laid down a tile drain to serve as a sewer from his house. When he was moving to another place the neighbours found him lifting the tiles, claiming they were moveable fittings!

THE SNOWBALL

141

THE SNOWBALL

Calum nan Croig was once reminiscing about his later years, when he and his wife were living in a little cottage at the foot of Ben Buie, at the other end of the island. There had been a heavy fall of snow on the hills, an uncommon occurrence in the mild climate of the place. This day, when his wife was away visiting a neighbour, Calum looked up at the white slopes of the Ben, and had an irresistible urge to try to revive the days of his youth by climbing to the top among the snow.

Yes, he said, he was still pretty spry and got on just fine, taking his time, of course. At the top, the spirit of mischief came back to him and he began to roll one of those big snowballs and push it over the edge, just for fun. It grew bigger and bigger as he rolled it, and he could hardly push it the last few feet to the edge of the drop, where it finally teetered over. Down it went, bounding out of sight among the slopes and corries, getting bigger and bigger all the time as it kept picking up the thick soft snow along a widening path.

Then, as Calum said, 'After a bit I took my way down again to the foot of the hill. But, oh, the place looked different, with snow lying in great heaps; in fact, I couldn't see the cottage for it. After digging for a while I came across a fine stag in the snow — then another — then a sheep or two — then a few more stags and hinds and sheep as I went on, all picked up by the snowball as it rolled down the hill. And oh, the rabbits and hares! Any amount!

'By the time I had dug out the house I had a pile of fifty deer on one side of me and a stack of ninety-nine sheep on the other; but I wassn't able to hide any of them, for up came the keeper and the shepherd to give me a hand. It wass very bad luck. Of coorse, I never told them how it had happened — and I managed to hide the one hundred and thirty eight rabbits and hares under the hay in the byre and sold them on the quiet later on. That wass something, too, I neffer let on to my wife.

'But when she got home in the evening and I wass telling her aal about it, "Oh," she says, quite angry, "Were you not the great fool. Surely you could haf kept back even one wee stag or a sheep; they would neffer miss it in that lot. And ninetynine sheep inteet! Could you no' haf made it the even hundred?"

' "Now, now," I says to her, "Surely you would not be making a liar out of me for the sake of one sheep?" '

RABBITS

Rabbits used to be a useful, if monotonous, addition to the menu of the islanders. A minister, visiting his parishioners, called on the man of the house to give thanks at the end of a meal of the inevitable stewed rabbit. This is how he expressed his feelings:

'Rabbits young and rabbits old,
Rabbits hot and rabbits cold,
Rabbits tender and rabbits tough,
I thank the Lord I've had enough'

Incidentally, the first rabbits ever seen in the island of Mull were located on the green *machair* above Calgary sands. No-one knew where they had come from, and at first they were a source of fear and wonder until they spread to every corner of the island, and their value became appreciated.

THE FALSE TEETH

Alisdair Susie lived in a little house with his mother and aunt. He had never plucked up courage to ask any girl to marry him; no, that would have meant a new and unknown way of life, and Alisdair was contented with what he had — two old *cailleachs* to wait on him hand and foot. But there was one snag; the way they talked. The chins wagged all day and the clash of tongues sometimes sent him running out of the house to enjoy the peace and quiet of the byre, with the slow quiet movements and rich rumblings of the three sleek Ayrshire cows. Never could he get a word in edgeways, so he gradually retired behind a wall of silence.

However, there came the morning when he was to go to the ferry with his mother to see her safely on the boat for a trip to Glasgow to see relatives. The alarm clock stopped, they all wakened late, and after a desperate rush they just managed to catch the early morning bus for the ferry.

But here was the strange thing. From the minute they left the house, Alasdair Susie began to talk as if he couldn't stop! In the bus, where of course he was known to everyone, they all stared at him astonished and anxious in case he was in a fever and needed the doctor. The more he talked, the quieter his mother became.

It was at the gangway that his talk came to a sudden end, just as his mother was going on board. 'I don't know what happened with my teeth this morning,' he said to his mother, 'For I haf been wearing yours aal the time. We must haf put in the wrong ones in the hurry.'

So they switched teeth under the eyes of the curious onlookers, and everything came back to normal. Alisdair Susie stood silently as the boat backed out, and the echoes of his mother's tongue were still audible as she sailed out of sight.

THE MIDGES OF MULL

Neil Munro gave a masterly description of the West Highland midges in the words of the legendary Para Handy. I suspect, however, that his familiarity with the indigenous Hebridean midge was rather superficial. After all, you have to live on the islands and know the peple before they will confide in you and tell you — fearfully, and looking round for an eavesdropping midge —of their personal experiences.

My most personal experience was one still, damp evening I inadvertently left an unopened tin of meat outside the entrance of my tent when I was camping up at the Lochs. In the morning I found it riddled with holes and polished out like silver by the hungry midges. You had to part them like heavy curtains to see outside the flap. These, however, were just the small ordinary midges. They were easily ejected from the tent by an occasional drag at a pipeful of Thick Black, which they loathed so much they shot out through the walls of the tent leaving holes of light which had to be patched before the rain came on.

Campers on the island without this local knowledge were pestered by these smaller midges sent in by the big ones to identify the most succulent blood groups. If this was satisfactory, the big ones would then lift the flap and go in for a feed. They didn't bother to carry off the campers themselves in case the really big midges got wind of this source of nourishment.

I was told the story of a freshly killed stag found hidden in a most unusual place in the middle of the bogland up the glen near the village. This gave us a topic of speculation for days in our busy street. The answer was finally provided by a shepherd at Drumtighe. One Saturday night, he said, just after closing time, when he was on his way home he saw this big midge, large even for our island, attack a stag, kill it and carry it down to this place in the boglands. Just before it began to eat the stag its attention was distracted by a jumbo jet plane passing over high up. Shortsightedly mistaking the plane for another midge coming to investigate, it took off to intercept, but on discovering its mistake it returned, but quite forgot where it had left the stag.

No, when Para Handy said the midges would bite through corrugated iron to get at you, he was a master of understatement. Only the risk of damaging the local tourist trade and the respect of local confidences prevent me from discussing the subject to its logical conclusion.

OLD TALES

FROM

THE GAELIC

THE FAIRY LOVER

Once upon a time there lived in the island a man called Donald MacRuairidh Bhain — Son Of Fair Roddy. Although married happily to an attractive wife, he developed the habit of rising every night after they had gone to bed and when his wife was asleep, and disappearing on some mysterious errand. No-one could tell where; but Donald began to waste away to a shadow of his former self.

At last the rumour spread that he was having a love affair with a fairy woman who had laid a spell on him. So a knowledgeable old woman broke the news to his wife and advised her to get something pertaining to the Gospels, a copy of the New Testament for instance, and tie it round her husband's neck after they had gone to bed. This she did, and sure enough, Donald settled happily to sleep for the first time since the fairy had laid her spell on him.

The fairy woman, wondering what was keeping Donald from their usual meeting, came to his bedroom window and looked in, but when she caught sight of him she cried out: 'Oh, there you are safely, Donald, with that lovely flame round your neck,' — and thus speaking, she vanished and left Donald in peace.

But there is a sequel to this story. Many, many years later —and Donald was an old man by this time — a travelling merchant with a pony and cart of goods came to a ford across the burn they call the *Abhuinn Tuil Ghall* (scene of the feud between the Mackinnons and the Macleans) when journeying between Mishnish and Quinish. His pony refused to cross, or even to set a foot in the water in spite of the exhortations of the merchant. Infuriated, the man at length caught the bridle of the pony and shouted: 'I'll get you across in the name of the Three Persons of the Trinity, though the Devil in Hell was here!'

Hardly had he spoken than a little old wife whom he had not seen rose suddenly on the other side of the burn and called out: 'If Donald MacRuairidh Bhain had said that to me the first night we met I wouldn't have troubled him for so long.' With that the fairy woman disappeared, the spell was broken, and the pony crossed willingly to let the merchant continue his journey.

THE YOUNG MAN'S TALE

There once stood a bothy beside the shore at an inlet of the sea, where the men and young fellows used to meet for a *ceilidh* on the long dark evenings, and maybe share a drop of home-made spirits from the big still in the cave that lay under the cliffs a few miles away. Stories were told and songs were sung and time passed with fun and banter round the peat fire that was kept burning in the middle of the floor. When it came to storytelling there was an unwritten rule they always observed. Everyone gathered in a ring round the fire, with the man of the house at the head. Starting with him, every person had to tell a story when his turn came, or be dragged out by the others and dipped in the burn that flowed past the house.

Now, one night, when it came to the turn of one of the young men, he was so tongue-tied that he just couldn't think of anything to say, and the others began to close in for the usual horse-play. However, the man of the house took pity on him and called out that before he told his story he should go out and stuff some hay into a hole in the wall to stop the draught that was coming through. Nothing loath, the young man hurried out to do the job. But when he had finished and glanced out to sea, he was shocked to observe a full-rigged ship speeding in before the wind straight for the rocky shore.

Running down to the rocks he pushed off a small boat that lay there with the oars in it, and rowed out with all his strength to warn the crew of their danger.   But hardly had he cleared the shore than the wind veered round and the ship turned away safely and disappeared.   But the rowing boat, caught now in the rising off-shore wind, was slowly driven out to sea before the squalls, in spite of the frantic efforts of the rower.   Soon he was out in the wide waters, drifting helplessly before the great waves of the ocean, his one objective being to keep the boat from capsizing.   Islands loomed up and moved past.   He heard the waves pounding on the cruel rocks of unseen coasts, driving him on and on for a whole day before the wind until in the falling darkness of another evening he came into the shelter of a little narrow bay where he stepped exhausted but safe on the shingle of a strange beach.   He had just enough strength left to pull up the boat and make it secure.

Seeing a light shining across a narrow *machair* above the bay he went up and found himself in front of a trim cottage, where he knocked at the door.   It was opened by a good-looking young girl who asked him to come in, in an accent that was quite new to him.   Beside her stood an elderly woman, her mother.

They soon exchanged their stories, and when he was fed and rested the young man discovered he had been driven all the way to the north coast of Ireland.   The man of the house had died just a week before, leaving the mother and daughter with the heavy work of digging their piece of ground and catching fish from the boat they kept down at the bay.   The young man fell in love with the girl the minute he saw her, and after a fortnight they agreed it would be a fine arrangement for them to get married, with mother in the house to help and him to do the fishing and work the land.   And so it came about that they all lived happily together for five years, with a child being born every year.   Then after the fifth year came tragedy.

He was out fishing one day when the wind came roaring out of the south-west. It was impossible for him to set sail or take to the oars, and once again he was driven out to sea, but this time in the direction from which he had come five years before, blinded by the spindrift, until after a long time the boat grounded on the black sand of a familiar cove. All the old landmarks were around him; the familiar hills stood behind. In fact, when he had made the boat fast and walked up to the bothy, he was astonished to see sitting round the fire the very same people who had been there five years ago when he had left.

Still in a dazed condition, when the old man asked him if he had fixed the draught, and if he had now thought up a story, the young fellow said yes, and began to tell them what had happened since he stepped out of the bothy five years before, and how he had been lucky and unlucky, but how he just could not understand what had happened. He was greeted with clapping and cheering, for it was the best story they had heard in a long time — until the man of the house held up his hand, and a silence fell as he rose to his feet.

'Do you not see his clothes are soaking,' he said, 'And the sea-salt thick upon them? The second sight has fallen on this man that he could live five whole years in the five minutes he was outside. It was a vision — not a story he was making up.'

The vision stayed with the young man as he went home to his father's croft; and ever after he was a sad and withdrawn man, sad and sorrowing for the wife and children he had left across the sea in Ireland.

DEAF JOHN

Were you ever hearing the story of the man who came to be known as Deaf John? He lived all by himself in a little thatched place near the sea, scraping a bare living from a few bits of ground among the rocks and some fishing from a boat he kept tied up in a sheltered cove. This was a long time ago, in the days when there were still pirates — like Ailean nan Sop, and some of the Danes — raiding the islands of the Hebrides.

One day when he was out fishing beyond the skerries a strange craft bore down on him and before he could raise the anchor and escape to the safety of the narrow channels among the reefs known only to himself, he was overtaken and found himself in the hands of a gang of cruel pirates. After they had ransacked his poor little boat and taken away the few fish he had caught, they stove in the boat and sank it. He was dragged on board the pirate galley and before the captain. 'Now, we are going to kill you; but we'll give you the choice of death by the knife or being thrown into the sea closed up tight in a barrel. Which is it to be?'

John knew there was no use in pleading for his life, so after some thought he asked the pirates if they would shut him up in the barrel and throw him in the sea. 'But as my last request', said John, 'Will you just make a small hole in the barrel so that I can breathe for at least a little time longer.' They agreed to do this, and John was coopered up and thrown over the side. However, he had managed to hide his knife, so at once, crouched in the barrel, he kept the hole above the water and began to whittle away at it.   Slowly he cut away at the tough wood until at last he had made a hole large enough for him to thrust first his hand, then his arm through it.

Now, this had taken a long time, and the barrel had drifted with the tide for many miles, until it was left stranded among the rocks of a strange shore.   But how could John escape from his cramped prison?

On looking through the hole he had managed to cut, he saw a number of cattle grazing along the tidal rocks on a certain type of seaweed they find there.   Presently a huge bull with widely spreading horns came so close that John was able to reach out, grab its tail and pull the end of it inside the barrel.   The startled beast gave a great bellow of rage and fright and went charging away up to the *machair,* dragging the barrel, bouncing and smashing from rock to rock, hammering and bruising poor John inside, who nevertheless held on grimly to the tail as he shouted for help in the Gaelic.

Up on the fields the people were working; but terrified by the sight of their maddened bull dragging behind it a bouncing barrel from which came a human voice shouting for help, they thought they were seeing a manifestation of witchcraft, and fled into their houses and barred the doors.   However, the bull, exhausted at last, came to a halt, and one man, bolder than the rest, ventured cautiously near to see what the mystery was.   John saw him through the opening and begged him to come and let him out, assuring him that it was just a very ordinary man that was cooped in the barrel.

So the man came up and after hearing John's story he set about breaking open the barrel and releasing the unfortunate prisoner. When he had recovered from his terrible experience John settled in the community and took up a new life.   But the confinement and bruising in the barrel had left him stone deaf, and evermore he was known to everyone as Deaf John.

THE UNFORTUNATE BATTLE

In the old days of clan life, many ceremonies were performed that had come down from the times of the Vikings, such as *Teine Eiken* or oaken fire, for charming away cattle diseases. Some go much further back, to the days when a pagan people raised the standing stones and stone circles and held rites or festivals to welcome the return of the sun, or the solstices; when perhaps the old worn cup-marked rocks have seen orgies and caught the blood of victims under the knives of the Druid priests. But more happy is one strange old tradition whose origin is unknown and which is itself now unknown — although on the occasion to be described the festivities ended in an inter-clan brawl.

The story, in the original Gaelic, describes how in days gone by, the clan folk observed two special days in the year as festivals, called Great Christmas and Little Christmas. The night of Little Christmas, known as *Oidhche Challuinn* (New Year's Eve) was marked by this old and special ceremony which was followed by rejoicing, and friendship and which was generally shared by every member of the community.

For the ceremony, a sheep was killed, then skinned whole except for a small patch of skin and fleece left on the animal's chest. This was then stripped clean of wool and carefully cut out, and was then called the New Year Token. The men and boys gathered together at a certain time, then, carrying the Token with them, and each person with a stick in his hand, they began to visit all the houses. The whole company walked three times round each house *deisel*, or clockwise (the lucky direction) striking the wall with their sticks and reciting certain verses that translate something like this: *'Oh Hogmanay; oh fine yellow sticks; strike the skin on the wall; old woman in the corner, old wife in the graveyard, another old wife by the fire, rise and open to us.'*

Further, each man had to improvise a verse at the door before it would be opened to him — any kind of doggerel would do: *'Get up kindly woman, and fine young maiden. Be generous at Hogmanay; give to us, as in days gone by, the smooth curded cheese hidden away for the occasion; but if you have none, meat and bread will do.'*

Then the door was opened and the men and boys went in. Accompanied by much merriment the Token was produced, lightly singed in the fire and then formally presented to the oldest woman in the house. After she had sniffed it, she handed it to the next person and then from hand to hand round the whole company. After that they settled down to feasting and enjoyment.

Now, this glad occasion was observed not only within townships but between whole districts. The dispute which gave rise to the title of this Tale arose in the days when the Mackinnons owned the lands of Mishnish and the chief stayed at Erray, just north of Tobermory. The custom was that on New Year's Day the Mackinnons and the Macleans of Torloisk (whose seat lay about twelve miles from Tobermory) used to visit each other and exchange hospitality and gifts.

This time the Mackinnons were the first to visit, and the Macleans gave them the most generous hospitality over at Torloisk, with every possible selection of food and drink, and even the present of a herd of cattle to take home with them. In turn, the Macleans came over to Mishnish, expecting at least reasonable hospitality, but all they received from the Mackinnons was the ordinary rather sparse fare normally provided at table, and no gifts at all.

Disappointed and incensed by this display of meanness, the Macleans promptly seized the cattle they had gifted to the Mackinnons and took the road back to Torloisk. However, the Mackinnons would have none of it, and a body of them followed their late guests and confronted them in a glen between Dervaig and Tobermory, beside the burn running northwards into Loch Mingary, known as *Abhuinn Tuil Ghall*. Feelings ran high, hot words were exchanged, and soon the dirks and broadswords were drawn. In the end, seven of the Mackinnons — and they had not even been among the guests at Torloisk — were lying dead. For this reason the name of the fight that should never have taken place has come down as 'The Unfortunate One.' At a crossroads of old tracks near the burn, not far from the present road, several low mounds are pointed out as the place where the seven unfortunate Mackinnons were buried.

ST. COLUMBA ON WOMEN

This quotation is attributed to St. Columba, when he banished women and cows from the sacred island of Iona:
'Far am bi bo bithidh bean;
Is far am bi bean bithidh molluchadh.'
'Where there is a cow there is a woman;
And where there is a woman there is mischief'

THE LEAPS OF THE GHILLIE REOCH

As you travel along the roads in the island you will see many little cairns. Some are on the hilltops or at the summit of road ascents, marking the achievements of walkers in getting there, each leaving a stone to mark his relief. Some mark the halting places of funerals in the old days, when the coffin was carried by bearers, or on a cart, over the long miles to the ancient graveyards. At every halting place each of the mourners added a stone to make a little cairn — you will still see a number of these exactly at the fourth milestone beside the loch on the Dervaig road, now deeply sunk in the heather. Some commemorate incidents, like McLucas's cairn above the Tostarie hill, the Pedlar's cairn in Strathcoil — and so on. There is one inconspicuous triangle of three little cairns lying in a boggy hollow beside a lay-by on a wide bend just over the summit of the Achnadrish hill as you are going to Dervaig. These are said to mark the leaps of the Ghillie Reoch.

This Ghillie Reoch, or Reddish Fellow, was a Mackinnon of Mishnish, a great athlete and an expert swordsman, whose services were much in demand during inter-clan raids. One day when he was all on his own at this very spot, he was surprised and set upon by a raiding party over from Coll, who were bent on paying back old scores, and they gleefully set about eliminating this stout member of the Mackinnon clan. Expert swordsman though he was, and nimble on his feet, he found himself hemmed in by sheer numbers, until his only hope of saving himself was to take the first of his three great leaps, one of thirty feet if it was an inch. The Coll men were quick to follow him up, and again he could only win clear by taking another leap of about the same distance. But the numbers around him were too great to be avoided, and he gave his final gigantic leap, and backwards at that from a standing start, of forty-five feet, right through the ranks of his attackers and back to his starting point. The three places from which he took off were each subsequently marked by a little cairn.

Anyway, this display of agility so incensed the chief of the men from Coll that he made the great mistake of hurling his battle axe at the elusive Ghillie Reoch, leaving himself defenceless — whereupon the Mackinnon man darted in and dispatched him with a cunning sword thrust through the body. Seeing their leader dead, the Coll men lost heart, and leaving the Ghillie Reoch master of the field, they withdrew down the hill to their galley in Loch Mingary, carrying with them the body of their chief.

Stones marking earlier cairns on the same spot have sunk deeply into the peat, certainly for hundreds of years, as I have found by probing with an iron rod. Some noteworthy incident is certainly commemorated here, and what better tradition can be preserved than the story of the Three Leaps of the Ghillie Reoch?

THE FIELD OF THE ENGLISHMAN

THE FIELD OF THE ENGLISHMAN

I wonder how many people, even local people, know the story
behind the name *Dal na Sasunnach* — The Field of the Southerner
or Englishman? This has been the locus every August for the
Mull and Morvern Agricultural Show — Salen Show, for short —
which has been going on now since when it began as a horse and
trading fair. The place is conveniently sited near the junction of
the main roads in the island, beside the estuary of the fine little
salmon river, the Aros, overlooked by the massive ruins of Aros
Castle, once an important cultural centre and a stronghold of the
Lords of the Isles. *Dal na Sasunnach* is linked with two
seemingly unconnected affairs through an English soldier — the
McArthur School of Piping in the island of Ulva, and the visit of
Lord Ochiltree's punitive fleet to Aros Bay in 1608.

McArthur, head of the piping school, was a most talented
exponent of the pipes. As a young man he had served the long
apprenticeship of a dedicated piper at Boreraig, in Skye, under the
most famous pipers of all time — the MacCrimmons. Neil
Munro, in *'The Lost Pibroch'*, gives a romantic description of the
art of piping. *'To the making of a piper go seven years of his own
learning and seven generations before. If it is in it will out.....if
not, let him take to the net or the sword. At the end of his seven
years one born to it will stand at the start of knowledge, and
leaning a fond ear to the drone, he may have parley with old folks
of old affairs.....he can stand by the cairn of kings, ken the colour
of Fingal's hair and see the moon-glint on the hook of the Druids.'*

McArthur was sent to Skye as a protege of the Marquis of Staffa and became an inspired pupil, quick to learn. So much so, in fact, the MacCrimmon himself became quite jealous of his talents and always arranged to send the youth on an errand when he himself was rehearsing some special composition. One day, however, McArthur loitered within earshot and overheard the playing of a very special air, which he memorised and played before his tutor at the first opprtunity, much to MacCrimmon's embarrassment. Afraid that word of his restricted teaching would reach the ears of the influential Marquis of Staffa, MacCrimmon admitted that the youth was a genius and began to teach him all he knew. In due course, McArthur returned to Ulva where he set up the college of piping that became second only to that at Boreraig.

Again, in the year 1608, a fleet under Andrew, Lord Ochiltree, set sail from Ayr under the orders of the Privy Council of Scotland to subdue the *'Rebellious and insolent persons inhabiting the Northern and Western Isles of the Kingdom committing certain barbarous villainies on each other without reference to God or Law.'*

After a stormy passage, interrupted to discipline the Clan Donald in Islay, and the Macleans of Duart, the admiral anchored in Aros Bay. Local chiefs were tricked into coming on board the flagship by an invitation to dine and hear an address by the Bishop of the Fleet; but as soon as they were below decks they were placed under guard and the fleet set sail for the south. In due course the chiefs were allowed to return home on providing sureties for their good behaviour and by signing the Statutes of Iona which did much to pacify the more unruly elements in the Hebrides.

All this is the background of the story of *Dal na Sasunnach.* The Englishman in the story was a soldier in the units carried on board the fleet. He happened to be on shore when the ships weighed anchor and departed so suddenly, and he found himself alone and stranded. Good-natured and adaptable, he remained in the district and was accepted by the community, becoming a farm worker. As time went on, he became aware that he possessed an astonishing talent — a love for the pipes, a natural speed on the fingering and an uncanny memory for all kinds of pipe music. Doubtless that was what attracted him into the service of Mc-Arthur of the Ulva piping college, now a grown man and living at the time at Ballygown, just across Loch Tuath from Ulva on the Torloisk side.

The Englishman, as befitted a common farm hand, always walked behind McArthur when in his company — '*in his tail*', as it was called. Now, McArthur was in the habit of carrying his stick behind his back and using it as an imaginary chanter on which he constantly practiced the fingering of his compositions. Any viewer would realise that this 'chanter' was in fact being fingered upside down, yet this was no deterrent to the Englishman, who watched closely the manner of fingering and automatically memorised it. He used to practice over and over again in secret on a length of stick and sometimes on a borrowed chanter when he was watching the sheep. His favourite place was within the sound of the Eas Fors, where the notes of his chanter were drowned by the roar of the cataracts.

There was one classical pipe tune, '*The Battle of the Birds*', (now lost to posterity, like the Lost Pibroch mentioned by Neil Munro) which McArthur found was a challenge even to his ability. Over and over again he fingered it on the stick behind his back, closely watched by the Englishman when he was in his tail. Seemingly this man mastered the intricacies as fast as his master; and one day, proud of his secret and deciding to come into the open and win the praise of McArthur, he borrowed a set of bagpipes.

Now it so happened that on that very day McArthur had arranged to give a rendering of this unique air to a critical and select audience he had invited to Ballygown. What was his rage and mortification to see the unfortunate Englishman, all unconscious of the enormity of his offence, come out on the knoll overlooking the assembled guests giving a perfect rendering of *'The Battle of the Birds'*.

Forgotten by McArthur was the understanding shown to him in his youth when he had stolen the thunder of the great MacCrimmon of Skye. Drawing their dirks, McArthur and his sons rushed up to silence the ill-fated piper and wipe out the insult. The poor man, suddenly finding himself friendless and hunted in a savage land, fled instinctively to the only sanctuary he could think of, his landing place at Aros Bay, twelve miles away, pursued by the McArthurs. Here, in the field that bears his name, his pursuers caught up and wiped out the unintentional insult in blood.

Perhaps at some future Salen Show, you will spare a thought for the unfortunate Englishman (or he might have been a southern Scotsman) who was put to death in that field for no other reason than that he was a born piper. *'If it is in, it will out.'*

THE KEEPER OF THE CATTLE

THE KEEPER OF THE CATTLE

In the old days, before walls or fences were ever thought of, the cattle of a community used to be guarded from straying or being 'lifted' by thieving neighbours by a man appointed to the job. Quite an important responsibility, for the wealth of the people lay in their herds of kyloes, or black cattle, forefathers of our picturesque modern Highland cattle.

Over at Haunn, where then there were fine grazing lands,there was one very conscientious Keeper of the Cattle, Hector by name. However, one day,when things appeared to be quiet, he went down to the rocks under the cliffs for an hour or two to catch some fish. When he returned to his charges, he learned to his mortification that in his absence three MacKinnon bothers had come over the hills from Mishnish and 'lifted' the best of the cattle.

Hector thought that if he hurried he could still intercept the thieves, slowed up as they would be by the cattle. Now, he was an expert archer — which makes me think the incident took place in the 16th century, for it was then, during the Wars of Montrose, that the bow and arrow was still being used in the Highlands. Anyway, Hector picked up his bow, but could only find three arrows. Thus armed, he hastened after the MacKinnons.

They, in their turn, had made good time from Haunn, and stopped at a little well near Ensay for a drink of water. The well was known ever since as *Tobar na Piobaire,* or the Well of the Piper, for here Hector loosed an arrow from concealment and

166

killed the first of the thieves, who happened to be a good piper. The other brothers hurried on, keeping where possible to open ground where Hector would be at a disadvantage; but by running hard round the other side of a hillock he reached a position where he let fly his second arrow and pierced the second brother through the heart.

It was evening now, and darkness falling, so the third brother was able to reach a great tangle of rocks and hide among them, abandoning the cattle. Hector, however, still feeling guilty at having failed to look after the cattle, was determined to eliminate the third thief as a lesson to all others, so all night he hid at the edge of the little cliff among the rocks, cold, hungry and weary, motionless below the edge of the skyline where the man below could not see him. So, when morning came, the remaining MacKinnon could see or hear no sign of his pursuer, thinking he had given up and returned home, so he came boldly out from his place of hiding in the rocks, and even thought he might still take the cattle with him, for they had not moved in the night.

But just at that, up rose the figure of Hector against the sky above, and let fly with his remaining arrow. Its flight was true, and the last MacKinnon dropped lifeless. Then Hector came down from his post, rounded up the cattle, and quietly drove them back to Haunn. Here the people had given him up for dead at the hands of the three powerful MacKinnon brothers. Ever after he was held in even greater esteem as the Keeper of the Cattle.

HOW THEY DODGED
THE KING'S MEN

Throughout the Highlands and Islands, in corners whose remoteness and inaccessibility defied the searches of the preventative officers, or King's Men, as they were known, the distilling of illicit spirits flourished with impunity from the seventeenth century onwards, when a tax was first imposed. The lairds winked at the practice, for it brought hard cash into the community, and allowed rents to be paid in money instead of produce or services. This ended in the 1820's, when it was enacted that lairds were to be held jointly responsible along with the operators on the lairds' lands.

The foundations of many of those old stills can still be seen to this day if you know where to look in caves and old ruins. The following story is connected with what must have been a giant still that operated in a cave in the lower cliff below Glacgugairidh, between Treshnish and Torloisk, a place where you can still see fragments of the staves of old kegs at the inner end of the cave. It was cunningly made; a trickle of water had been diverted to fall over the mouth of the cave and cool the 'worm' from the 'Black Pot'. A turf dyke had been built across the entrance to conceal the glow from the eight feet wide furnace, whose smoke merged into the cliffs above and vanished. A bridle path had been cleverly contoured into the steep gully in the cliff for use of the pack ponies. The spirits made here must have been of a high quality, for the fishermen who used to run the still up to the middle of the 19th century used to row and sail their boats with a load of their produce all the way over to Ireland.

Now, this time they started off bound for Tiree with a load of kegs, but on reaching the open water they were observed by a preventative cutter that changed course to intercept them. At once the fishermen crowded on all sail and with the wind now behind them they made for the distant islands of Coll and Tiree. In spite of their efforts, the cutter was slowly gaining on them by the time they were off the island of Tiree.

Rounding the point and entering the little bay, the fishermen saw waiting for them a great crowd of people who had been excitedly watching the chase. Hardly had the boat grounded on the sandy beach than dozens of people came running down. The kegs of spirits were whisked away and into safe hiding places. The boat was lifted bodily out of the water and carried up the beach, where they set it down among the boats of the village, nearly all the same design of fishing boat, above high-water mark. Water was thrown over all the boats to make them more difficult to identify, and while all this was going on, other people were driving the cattle across the sands so that the only marks to be seen were hoof marks.

Hardly was all this done and the people dispersed to their houses or to their work than the cutter came tearing round the point, and presently a party of the King's Men under an officer came hurrying ashore. But all they could see was two old men sitting mending a net.

'Did you see a boat come in a short time ago?' called the officer; but the two old men knew no English and just kept on working. Then one of the King's Men asked them the same question in the Gaelic, and the men looked up astonished.

'A boat?' they said. 'There are only our own boats here, as you can see for yourselves, and nobody has been out in them. Just look for yourselves, there are only the two of us here at the nets.'

So the mystified King's Men looked round, and right enough the boats were all drawn up in a row on the beach, and they could see only one or two people hoeing the potato drills far up above the *machair.*   There was nothing to see on the sandy beach but the tracks of the cattle, and they were quietly grazing over on the other side.

'This is very strange,' said the officer to his men.   'We certainly saw the boat coming round the point there, and there is no sign of her here.   She must have hugged the shore close in and gone on.   Come on — we're wasting time; back to the boat and make sail and we'll maybe catch them yet.'

So away sailed the cutter in a great hurry, looking into every bay and cove as it flew past — but they never caught the fishermen or their boat.   In Tiree that night there was laughter and merrymaking, and the Mull men were the heroes!

THE GHOSTS OF HOSGEIR

THE GHOSTS OF HOISGEIR

Another story originating in the illicit distilling of whisky comes this time from the south end of Mull, where a very successful still was run by three neighbours. When they had gathered a big enough supply, they used to row out to the islands, Coll, Tiree, and elsewhere, where their product was much appreciated. One night — what they used to call 'Little Christmas' — they were returning from Tiree after delivering a seasonable consignment, and were quite close to Mull, when an east wind carrying a great blizzard of snow suddenly rose against them. They could make no headway at all in the darkness.

Blinded by the freezing snow they were at last obliged to turn and flee before the storm. Soon, two of the poor men became overcome by the freezing cold and icy spray and died where they sat, leaving the third man huddled at the stern oar trying to keep the stern into the wind. Perhaps the effort of doing this saved him. Hour after hour the boat drove on into the pitch blackness of the winter night until just after midnight the lone survivor heard the roar of surf dead ahead of him. Coming near rocks, where the waves were creaming white in the blackness, he managed to steer into the partial shelter of a projecting rock and looked for somewhere to land.

Just at that a voice called out from the direction of the big rocks —'Come this way.....' but hard on top of it came another shout from further on — 'NO, come THIS way.....' 'And who is that calling?' cried the exhausted man. 'I'm Mac Ille Ruaidh' (Son of the Red Fellow), came the response. Then still another voice cut in — 'No, No! Come over HERE!' 'And who are you?' 'Oh, I am the Mac Ille Dheirg' (also Son of the Red Fellow), came the response. But when the bewildered man heard a fourth voice imploring him to 'COME OVER THIS WAY,' and who called himself the Son of the Fair Fellow, he shouted back — 'Away you go, the whole lot of you. I'll come to where I heard the first man calling.' So saying, he eased the boat in that direction and was lifted by a wave on to a sloping rock that smashed the front of the boat but allowed him to scramble stiffly ashore. But although he called and called, he neither heard nor saw anything of the people who had been shouting at him.

When morning came he found himself marooned on what was no more than a big reef, with a pocket of earth and coarse grass on the top which the tide never reached. Here he dug a shallow hole with his knife that gave some shelter from wind and rain and snow, and there he endured until the storm passed away. When he crawled out of the hole he saw the hills of distant islands and the mainland glowing white with snow down to the edge of the sea, and the sky was blue and hard. He was entirely without food or drink, except for a slab of butter rolled up in a cloth in his pocket, and melted snow and rainwater on top of the rocks. He walked all along the reef when the tide was out looking for traces of living people, but not a human being could possibly have been there, especially in the face of the waves and storms of the previous day. The only safe landing place was where he had obeyed his instincts and pulled in the boat, which was now no more than a few broken planks, where the first voice had called to him.

He remained marooned on the reef from New Year's Day until Saint Peter's Day (29th June), surviving on shellfish, chiefly raw limpets which he gathered from the rocks with his knife, warming them in the sun when it became warmer, and swallowing them with a taste of the butter as long as it lasted. Every single night about midnight he was disturbed by the ghostly voices, shouting and screamings, as if people were drowning. It was so real that to begin with he used to start up and run to the edge of the rocks; but finding nothing tangible to account for the phenomenon he became tired of it all and in the end he just ignored it and stayed in his poor shelter.

On Saint Peter's Day he was seen at last waving frantically by a passing fishing boat. You see, they kept far off because of the hidden reefs, too far away as a rule to see him. They carried him over to Uist, where he was nursed back to health and cared for with such great kindness that he was soon back in full health, and the effects of his harsh and eerie experience were mellowed with the passing of time, athough he often puzzled over the reason for the ghostly voices, perhaps the spirits of a shipwrecked crew.

At last he was carried back to the south of Mull by a boat going that way. His wife, stricken with grief, had given him up as dead, and on the very day he returned she was selling up everything in the house to provide for her keep. Great was the relief and rejoicing at the return of even one man of the three who had been given up long since as lost, and the neighbours hastened to return all the household goods they had bought from the wife.

The reef on which he was cast up is called Hoisgeir, and lies over near the island of Canna, which gives some idea of the distance the boat had been driven on the night of the storm.

THE TWO HERDSMEN OF LOCHBUIE

THE TWO HERDSMEN OF LOCHBUIE

This story goes back probably to the 16th or 17th century, certainly to the great days of clan life when the chiefs had powers of life and death over their clansmen, when superstition was rife, and when keeps and castles, now in ruins, stood foursquare and resounded with song, music, story, or the clash of arms. It was translated to me by a friend, an old Gaelic scholar, who died not long ago. Although it loses much of its original nuances and asides, even in the poor medium of the English it is an amusing and tangled tale.

Eachann and Seumas were two herdsmen who looked after the cattle beasts of the chief of the MacLaines of Lochbuie, a stern fighting man whose old castle of Moy still stands above the rocky shore, where you can see the cleared channel where once the galleys were drawn up. The little cot houses of the two men lay quite near each other, and their two wives often looked in on each other for a gossip. One day Bean Eachann opened her neighbour's door and found her busy at the boiling of a pot over the peat fire.

'What have you got in the pot today?' she asked.

'Oh, I'm just making a drop of brochan for Seumas's dinner,' replied the other.

'And what kind of broth is it?'

'It's just some *dubh-brochan.*' (That was a simple broth consisting of oatmeal, water, and little else.)

'My, is he not the poor man,' commented Bean Eachann. 'Can you no' get more than that? Even a bit of meat to put in the brochan? Why, ever since I can remember, Lochbuie has given Eachann a whole ox for himself every year, and we are never without a piece of meat in the house.'

Bean Eachann thought for a minute. Then she announced to her downcast friend: 'I'll tell you what we will do. I'll send over Eachann tonight and he can plan with Seumas how to get one of the chief's oxen. It will never be missed.'

So that night Eachann and Seumas put their heads together and discussed methods of getting an ox for Seumas.

'We daren't ask Lochbuie for one,' said Eachann, 'For he is a hard man; so we will just have to steal one. But this is what we will be saying if we are asked so that we will not be telling a lie: you do the stealing of the ox, and then bring it over to me; then if anybody asks us, you can swear, "I didn't take it home," and I will swear, "I didn't take it from the fold," which will be truth.'

So the very next night away went the two plotters to a wood not far from the cattle enclosure. Eachann went first, and when he was sure that everything was quiet and nobody about, he went round to the other side of the wood and lit a small fire, which was the sign to Seumas that the coast was clear. But as Seumas was slipping quietly down to the fold, he heard the voices of some men coming near, and their dogs began to bark, so he hid for a while. Although they moved on, he was still uneasy, and decided to go back and tell Eachann that they had better put off their plan for another night.

Now, that evening Lochbuie was entertaining a party of friends over at the castle. He was telling them how that day he had ordered a thief to be hanged from a tree at the edge of the wood — some miserable *truaghan* of a fellow with a big red beard. After the *usige beatha* had gone its rounds of the chief's table a few times, encouraging the boasters and heartening the timid, one of the guests wagered that there was not a man in the 'tail' of Lochbuie who would venture into the dark wood and come back to Moy Castle with a shoe off the foot of the hanging man.   There was a long silence.   Then big MacGillivray, one of the boatmen, when the nature of the wager had been explained to him, got up and swore that he would do this deed for the honour of his chief.

Now Seumas was still far away, hiding at the fold, when MacGillivray came into the wood where Eachann — who by the way had a fine red beard of which he was very proud — was warming himself at the fire as he waited for Seumas, all unconscious of the grim, dark corpse swinging at the end of the rope only a few yards away.   So when MacGillivray reached the place, he saw to his horror that what he took to be the red-bearded corpse was warming itself beside the fire.

'*A Chruitheir,*' he exclaimed, recoiling in horror, 'It is the corpse come to life that I am seeing,' and he went running back to the castle, where he panted out his story to the sceptical audience.

'Just as I said,' crowed the challenger, 'A lot of cowards you have in your tail, Lochbuie!'

As the chief glowered, not very well pleased, a crippled servant boasted: 'A fine lot you are!   If only I had my feet I would come back with the leg as well as the shoe!'

'Come on, then,' challenged MacGillivray, to put an end to the bragging, 'And I will put a good pair of feet under you.'

So he lifted the cripple on to his back and the two of them set out for the wood once again.   But right enough, on seeing what he thought could certainly be no other than the dead, red-bearded thief sitting by the fire, the panic-stricken cripple struggled to be off; but this time MacGillivray held on to him and stood his ground.

Just then Eachann, still waiting patiently for Seumas to join him, looked round and saw the dim figures.   Thinking it was Seumas at long last returning with the ox, he called out: 'Have you come back?'

'Yes,' answered MacGillivray nervously.

'And have you got him?'

'Yes.'

'And is he fat?' — but this was too much for Macgillivray: 'Fat or thin, here he is!' he screamed, and throwing the cripple towards the fire he took to his heels as if the Evil One was behind him — followed by the terrified cripple, hopping and scrambling on all-fours and bringing up the rear.

Poor Eachann, who was convinced now that he had been watched by the chief's men, that Seumas was taken, and that now the game was up, he might as well go straight to the castle, confess everything, and throw himself on the mercy of his chief.

Meanwhile, MacGillivray, still shaking with terror, had returned to the castle. 'Where is your companion?' they asked him, 'And did you get the shoe?'

'Indeed, and we did not!' he replied. 'It was indeed the hanged man sitting by the fire. He called out to me if the cripple was fat, so to save myself I threw him down and came away. By now he will have eaten the cripple.'

As he was finishing, in crawled the cripple, screaming that the man from the gallows was at his heels; so when Eachann came humbly to the door seeking admittance, he found it locked and barred, with sounds of panic and the clash of steel inside as the household prepared to repel the powers of evil. Eachann knocked and knocked for a long time, calling out that he was only one of Lochbuie's herdsmen. At last the door was opened a crack by the armed guards; Eachann was admitted and led before his chief.

After a great deal of explaining, and with due humility, Eachann unburdened his conscience. There was a wave of relief and a great deal of laughter at the expense of everyone concerned, and Eachann was allowed to go his way unpunished — although still puzzled by the whole affair, for nobody had mentioned the corpse hanging in the wood so near where he had been.

Now, all this time Seumas, empty-handed and disappointed, was slowly returning through the trees to tell Eachann of his lack of success. But as he came towards the fire he ran into the body of the thief swinging in the darkness. He was stricken with fright and despair, and when he saw the glint of the red beard he cried — 'Oh, poor Eachann, so they caught you when I was away, and there you are at the end of a rope. This is what comes to us for listening to those chattering wives of ours. The least I can do is to take you down and back to your wife.'

So Seumas cut down what he thought was the body of his friend and carried it on his back all the way to Eachann's house. There were great *ochones* and lamentations when Bean Eachann opened the door and saw what she thought was the body of her husband lying out there in the dark.

'Be quiet,' hissed Seumas; 'If we are not quick we'll all be hanged the same way if the chief finds out. Get me a spade and we'll bury him in the corner of the garden and maybe nobody will get to know.' So they dug a deep hole and covered up what they thought was the body of Eachann; whereupon Seumas hurried away to share his fears and troubles with his wife in his own house.

While all this was going on, Eachann, after his visit to the castle, was hurrying home much relieved at receiving so mild a rebuke from Lochbuie. To his surprise, he found his house door bolted, which was most unusual. He knocked and hammered in increasing exasperation, but his wife, cowering in bed dazed with fear and sorrow, was afraid to answer, thinking it was the chief's men come for her.

At last he roared out: 'Open the door! It's me, Eachann!'

This, of course, made matters worse. 'Oh, no!' she cried in superstitious terror. 'I'm not going to open the door to a hanged man. Away you go to your place back under the earth!'

Poor Eachann, thinking his wife had taken leave of her senses, turned and ran over to the cot house where by this time Seumas and his wife had settled down uneasily for the night behind locked doors. Again Eachann knocked and announced who he was; again the door remained barred. The bewildered man began to think there was some kind of *buidseachan* (curse, or evil spell) on him.

At last Seumas, from inside, fearful of the supernatural, quavered out: 'You'll no' get in here. I got enough of you earlier carrying you home on my back after I cut you down in the wood.'

'Is it you or me that is daft!' roared the angry Eachann. 'Get you a light and you will see I am no more hanged than youself!'

With shaking fingers Seumas lit a candle and held it up at the window, and by its light he could indeed see Eachann standing outside as large as life with no visible signs of hanging or interment about his person. So Seumas let him in, and along with his wife they made up the fire and discussed the whole tangled affair. They agreed to go together to the chief and throw themselves on his mercy, although they still knew nothing of the dreadful identity of the third man.

However, when the chief heard the whole story he laughed until he nearly choked. But it had been such an entertainment and they had made such an honest confession that he forgave them Every year after that Eachann and Seumas both received an ox from the chief's herd, so everybody finished up pleased — everybody but the poor *truaghan* hanged on the tree.

TALES OF THE

THE RESURRECTION MEN

MACABRE

182

THE RESURRECTION MEN

In summer, when I was a boy, the mile of dusty road between our house and the school or village was of never-ending interest. There was the Doctor's Spring to slake my thirst, the bridge over the little burn over whose parapet I cautiously peered at the trout in the pool below; the luscious brambles and wild strawberries in season, the wild flowers, the trees with their October harvest of hazel nuts.

But how it all changed in the dark of winter! Gloomy and wind-swept, haunted by ghosts described in the fireside stories; past the crossroads where the man drowned himself in the water tank; then, just short of the village, the cemetery, whose grey walls barely held back the crowding, humpy headstones. I still recall my fears when the lightning flashed in the darkness and reflected back in an unearthly fashion from polished tombstones, then the crash of thunder which might have raised the dead, gibbering, from their narrow beds just a yard or two on the other side of the wall.....

Within the old section of the cemetery one particular tombstone, now damaged and recumbent, lies near the wall at the top. Through the centre of it is a bullet hole caused by a rifle shot one night over a century ago. Before I tell you of the incident, let me give you the background.

You may be surprised to know that even late last century a strange and gruesome trade was being conducted surreptitiously in the island, as well as throughout the country. Away in Glasgow anatomists in the medical school were paying good money with no questions asked for nice fresh corpses supplied for dissection.

Why, you will still see preserved in some churches and cemeteries the 'mortsafes', the heavy iron cages that were placed over new graves to discourage the attentions of the grave robbers. Certain anonymous characters in the island were prepared to follow the ghoulish trade in the dark of the moon for a quick five-pound note; no-one knew their identity, although it was suspected that the local doctor, a bachelor who lived all by himself, was the go-between, the man who received the bodies and salted them into casks for transportation by sea to Glasgow.

When my father was a young man he sometimes joined the party of men who kept watch at lonely Pennygown cemetery for a week or two after a burial. After that the body would be safe from the attentions of the resurrectionists. In cold weather the party lit a fire of driftwood from the shore below in the lee of the cemetery wall, put up a tarpaulin for shelter, and passed the time with song and story — but always with an eye open and a gun handy.

It was a similar party of watchers in the old cemetery one night, with a full moon, who saw a couple of figures slinking towards the grave where an interment had just taken place. Raising the rifle, one of the watchers let fly, but missed the shadowy forms and instead scored a bullseye in the centre of the tombstone I mentioned earlier; and there lies the evidence to this day. The man who fired the shot was the grandfather of my friend who related the story. In point of fact, the man rashly set out in pursuit of the two figures, followed by the rest of the watchers; however he caught his foot between two tombstones, came down, and broke his leg: a thoroughly unsuccessful night for him. However, the story continues with a follow-up describing how the ghoulish practice was brought to an end.

I mentioned the local doctor as the suspected go-between in the corpse trade. Although no-one had any actual evidence, they visualised the tap at the doctor's back door, the men there with their clothes muddy and stained, with the long, canvas-wrapped bundle at their feet ready to slip in the moment the door opened, the hand extended to grab the five pound note (the standard payment), and not a word spoken.

Well, the watchers and their friends decided to settle the question once and for all: but they bided their time with patience until circumstances favoured them. The time came with a burial no-one had arranged to watch. The moon was just right. But what added the perfect touch to the plot was that on that very day a ship had called in at the bay for fresh provisions. Among the sailors to come ashore was the cook, a big black negro full of fun. So after fraternising and standing a few rounds, the plotters called this sailor to one side and unfolded a plan to him. In a minute they were helpless with laughter, and presently they slipped quietly out.

Just after midnight there came the tapping at the doctor's back door. A bit surprised, for there had been no hint that there was a job on, he lit a candle, pulled on an old dressing gown, and cannily opened the back door. The long bundle was pushed inside, the money accepted that the doctor held ready in his hand, and the figures departed.

The doctor decided to prepare the body for transportation there and then, so he dragged the bundle to the middle of the kitchen floor. The flickering candle on the corner of the table was throwing strange shadows and as he stooped over he almost imagined there was a movement under the sacking. Gripping the sack at the end where the head should have been, he was just about to slit through when a long shining steel blade came cutting through the canvas from the inside, followed by a huge fist gripping the knife, and after it a fearsome black face with rolling eyes and flashing white teeth as the fabric split right down.

Well, it was said afterwards by the lads who were watching, convulsed with laughter, behind the dyke just above the house, that the scream of fright the doctor gave set all the dogs in the district howling and awoke the whole village. He carried the back door with him and never touched the handle as he went out, and finished at the far end of the street cowering under the bed on which a highly respectable Kirk elder and his wife were in nocturnal repose. How the doctor explained it away afterwards is not recorded, but from then on the newly dead slept undisturbed in that corner of the island.

Still rolling on the ground with laughter, the plotters were joined by the black sailor carrying under his arm the sacking in which he had been wrapped. Not only had the plot exceeded all expectations, but they had the doctor's five pound note as well for a further celebration!

THE HAUNTED BUSHRANGER

THE HAUNTED BUSHRANGER

The house of Sunipol is an old substantial farm house standing at the edge of the cliff as you go along the side road from Calgary to Caliach, that wild headland in the north-west of Mull.   It has two widely differing claims to be of unusual interest.   First, the poet Thomas Campbell, who lived from 1777 to 1844 and duly became Poet Laureate, was here for two years in his early '20s — about 1800 — acting as tutor to the family.   The second concerns certain unexplained happenings around the building attributed to the ghost of a bushranger and the aborigines he murdered.

Mull, with its romantic associations, had a profound influence on the young poet, which can be seen in some of his greatest works later on in life.   He also wrote such poems as *Lord Ullin's Daughter* and *Glenara,* based on local folklore.   The former, well-known in our schooldays, describes the elopement of the daughter of Sir Alan Maclean of Knock with the young MacQuarrie, chief of Ulva's Isle, and their fate when escaping across the ferry.

Glenara, a lesser known poem, tells the story of the Lady Rock, a tidal reef off Duart Castle on which Lachlan Maclean, described as the 'only bad chief of the Macleans' marooned his wife in the hope that the rising tide would dispose of her.   Saved by a passing fishing boat, she duly returned to her father, the Duke of Argyll.   The poem goes on to describe the confrontation between the chief and his 'dead' wife, and the retribution that fell on him.

More creepy is the story of the hauntings and the Australian connection.   After much local research, it has been possible to piece the story together.   Last century, when Australia was in the early stages of development, the then tenant of Sunipol, Campbell by name (no connection with the present incumbent), went out to see for himself if there were any prospects of making some money. In a year or two he came back to Sunipol a wealthy man, having lined his pockets in some manner he would not disclose. Every few years, apparently when his funds were needing renewal, he would — as he said in the Gaelic — 'Take a leap over to Australia', returning later with more money than ever.

As time went on, strange happenings took place round the house. Stones, sometimes quite large ones from the shore down below, were found lying in the garden, sometimes hitting the walls of the house. My own father used to describe how during the tenancy of his father (my grandfather, who died there in 1905), stones kept appearing in the most unusual places. Further, there were reports of seeing the flitting shapes of little aborigines round the house, and after Campbell died there was something of a free-for-all in the ghost world between his and theirs after dark.

It would appear that out in Australia Campbell used to kill off the aborigines for their cattle, which he sold at enough profit to make him wealthy. At that time, too, there was a government bounty for every aborigine killed, so I would imagine that Campbell was a ruthless man who joined up with the bounty hunters and shared in the disposal of captured cattle and gear. It is said, too, that he used to waylay some of the gold prospectors returning from the diggings and rob them of their hard-won gold: hence his reputation as a bushranger.

By a coincidence, the tenant at Sunipol at present is also Campbell by name, although having no connection with the ghostly bounty hunter. In fact, the passing of time must have wearied the ghosts of their activities, for he has had no manifestations during his occupancy.

—————◄◆►—————

THE RAMSHORN CROOK

THE RAMSHORN CROOK

If you will go west of Oban and get to know the islands, you will find they have an atmosphere all of their own.   Something hard to put into words.   And yet, just think of the peoples that worshipped at the standing stones; or in the later chapels; who built the cairns and castles, and who lived and died in the old ruined villages in the hollows of the hills; it is not so hard to believe that echoes from the past can still be heard in this age of motor cars, television and car ferries.   If you bear with me, I'll tell you of a queer experience I had myself which will perhaps explain something of what I am trying to say.

Archie and me were back on another job in the island.   It was late in the day by the time we were finished and we were motoring back in a borrowed car that had seen better days.   In fact, it broke down when we were still five or six miles from the village.   It was a still evening, no wind, with the sunset glowing in the west and a full moon beginning to rise over the dark hills to the east.   We pushed the car on to a flat place beside the road and began to walk — something neither of us liked very much unless there was a good trout loch at the other end.   Archie reminded me about the old short cut through the hills somewhere nearby that would save us a mile or two; but it was so long since either of us had used it, and so seldom (and then always by daylight) that we had forgotten where it struck off the main road.   So when we came to a little cottage by the roadside we knocked at the door to ask the way.

It was opened by an old *cailleach* who looked like a witch the way the lamp was shining at her back, but she answered civilly enough in her cracked old voice:

'Yes, it will be just two miles from here to the village if you will be taking the path behind the house.   It goes straight up the hill and down the Bealach Dubh.'

She looked past us and kind of hesitated as if she wanted to say more; then she added — 'But maybe it would be far better tonight if you were to keep to the main road.'

The door was closing before we could say goodnight, or thank her, or even ask what she meant by the warning.   Well, we pushed past the broken-down gate held together with stack rope that led into the field and began to follow the path beyond.   It was easy enough to follow, worn by the sheep, rising steeply up the hill to the watershed, then dropping quickly between the dark cliffs of the Bealach Dubh.   The rising moon kept dodging between slowly drifting clouds, leaving patches of brightness and dark shadows. The black rocks were tilting above us and we walked through patches of coarse heather with the bleached stones of the path under our feet.   We came to a place where a few lonely trees stood up, with their branches twisted and whitened like skeletons by the fierce winter gales that howl up the pass from the sea.

It was just here that Archie and I both had a sudden feeling of uneasiness.   Away up above the rocks the sheep were bleating uneasily, and moving restlessly for no reason we could think of — unless it is getting near the lambing, we whispered to each other, for we didn't feel like talking out loud.   Without noticing it we had begun to quicken our steps; but in spite of the exercise we could not throw off a strange chill that seemed to have settled on us.

It was then I began to remember some of the stories of long ago we had been told down in the bar at the hotel; not all fairy tales either, as the locals assured us.   I was indeed glad to have Archie with me.   However. we felt more assured when we saw the distant lights of the village far round a shoulder of the hill.

Then all of a sudden, as the moon came sailing round the edge of a dark cloud, making our path as bright as day, we saw the big dog. It was trotting towards us in and out of the shadows of the bare twisted trees that lay along the ground like black snakes. It was a handsome collie dog, one of yon ones with an extra long nose and a white ruff round its neck, not a bit like the usual run of shepherds' dogs in the island. We called to him, snapped our fingers, even tried a few words of the Gaelic on him, but for all the attention he paid we just weren't there. He passed without a sound in the middle of the path not a yard from where we had drawn aside; not even the scuff of a loose stone under his feet, until he vanished behind a bank of long heather.

'Now, there's a queer thing,' exclaimed Archie in a hushed voice. 'Did you see the way his eyes were shining? He looked uncanny.'

'Ach, it's just somebody's dog away visiting,' I whispered back — just to reassure myself — 'I hope he won't be teaming up with another dog and having a go at the sheep.'

Archie wasn't saying any more. When I glanced at him a grue came over me, the way he had stopped and was staring down the path. My heart gave a jump when I saw a figure striding towards us like a man used to the hills. However, we relaxed when he came near, for it was a shepherd, a tall man with a fine set of whiskers, wearing homespun tweeds and some sort of raincoat slung over his shoulder. But what caught my eye was the most beautiful and unusual crook made of ramshorn that I have ever seen — and mind you, I should know, for many's the one I've tried my hand at myself. As he grasped it in the moonlight I could see clearly that it was carved like a leaping fish. He halted a few steps away and hailed us in the Gaelic.

'Well, boys, you're late on the road. Were you taking the short cut?'

We gave him a friendly greeting and told him how our car had broken down and how glad we would be to reach the village before closing time.

'Tach,' he remarked with contempt, 'I never trust these new-fangled machines they are talking about. Our own two feet is good enough.'

We laughed at what we thought was his litle joke, then mentioned the dog. 'That's a fine looking dog you've got. We saw him go by just a minute or two ago. Does he work as well as he looks?'

'Dog?' repeated the shepherd looking at us queerly; 'What dog?' — so we went on to describe the handsome collie.

'Yes,' he remarked thoughtfully after a pause, 'That is like Dileas right enough. But, man, what a strange thing you are telling me — in fact, how can it be, for Dileas was killed — oh, ten years ago, when he fell over the edge of the cliff up there just above us.'

The tall shepherd stood there sad and quiet, leaning on his stick, his face deeply hidden in the black shadows of his hat. Something about the figure, the bare cliffs and black shadows behind him in the moonlight, caused a great fear to come on Archie and me, and an urge to be gone from the place. As we turned to hurry away with a hasty 'Goodnight' he called after us:-

'*Beannachd leat.* Tell them all in the Maclean Arms I was asking for them.'

When we risked a quick look back he was gone — just a big cloud shadow where he had been.

To tell you the honest truth, we became panic stricken and took to our heels, tripping and falling over things hidden under our feet. A deathly stillness had come down. Not a sound any more from the sheep, not a rustle in the long grasses; nothing but the rattle of the little burn dropping near us among the stones. Don't laugh at me if I tell you it sounded as if it was rattling through dead mens' bones — it was no laughing matter for us at the time. Our hearts were thumping when we came panting down past the cemetery above the village where the moon was leaping and dancing on the polished tombstones — the way we were feeling it could have been the ghosts of the dead.

But ach, we were a bit ashamed of our fears when we found ourselves standing at last at the bar of the Maclean Arms with two short drinks and two long cold ones in front of us — and were we needing them! Big Duncan himself was serving at the bar.

'Duncan,' I said to him when there was a pause in the talking, 'Who is that fine big shepherd we met a wee while ago in the Bealach Dubh? He was asking for you all in here. Likely he would be in too much of a hurry to look in, for he went out of sight fast enough.'

'The big shepherd?' repeated Duncan thoughtfully.

'Yes, yes,' broke in Archie; 'You must know him fine. Long whiskers, an old kind of hat, and man! the most beautiful crook in his hand like a leaping fish. And — here's the strange thing. Just before we saw him we were passed by his dog — a real champion collie.....' and Archie went on to describe it.

'But that's not all,' I added. 'The queerest thing of all was that he said we must have been wrong, for his dog Dileas was killed on the cliff above us ten years ago.'

It was then that I became aware that the bar had fallen silent and all the folk had gathered round us listening to every word we were saying, even forgetting the drinks in their hands. Duncan was standing there behind the bar wiping the same patch of the counter round and round with the cloth in his hand as if he hardly knew what to say

'Well, well, well!' he came out at last. I'm not saying for one minute you didn't see all that. But stop you: would it be a crook shaped like a jumping salmon? Well, just you look carefully up there.'

High up on the wall above the bar, lying across a fine pair of antlers (to which I had never paid much attention before, treating them as part of the general decorations), I became aware for the first time of the details — and I would swear before a judge it was the very same crook as the one we had seen in the hands of the shepherd. It was a staff of dark hazel wood fitted into a leaping salmon so carefully carved in horn you could see the very scales.

'Would that be the crook you were seeing tonight?' continued Duncan. 'It belonged to old MacArthur, the shepherd at Cnocfuar. The dog you were seeing was his favourite dog Dileas: but the dog was killed when he fell over the cliff just above where you saw him in the Bealach Dubh, and ten years later MacArthur himself fell to his death at the very same place. It was one night — just about now — before the lambing, when he was up the hill seeing to the sheep. This bar was the last place he was ever seen alive. But that would be — oh — fifty years ago, when I was a boy, and I used to hear my father telling about it.'

TWO PIECES OF GOLD

TWO PIECES OF GOLD

I dare say if I had lived long ago I might have been one of those people embarrassed by having a touch of the second sight. However, with most of a lifetime spent away from the islands, a veneer of sophistication has covered over any manifestations. There have been times when I had an uneasy awareness, an unsuccessful groping for the explanation of some unaccountable occurrence, an intangible link with the past as difficult to recollect as to explain. That is, all but once; the one time I had a terrifying experience from which I emerged with no doubts at all that I had indeed been in the presence of some power of evil with its roots in the past. But wait you, and I'll tell you just what happened — and the evidence that puts it all beyond the bounds of a fanciful imagination.

With the sun blazing down day after day from cloudless summer skies — yes, it used to happen! — I decided to spend a few days of my holidays walking through the hills and tracks to my island. I took the train to a point beyond Lochailort on the Mallaig line (that scenic railway which but for stodgy remote control could be a major Scottish tourist attraction) and began walking, with no more than a light knapsack on my back and a hazel crook in my fist, heading for Kilchoan or Lochaline as my feet took me.

It was late in the evening when I came over the watershed and saw below me a wide bay whose jutting headlands seemed to cradle the setting sun. The golden heat of the day had given way to a cool evening breeze from off the sea, and behind me the blue spires and darkening corries of the high hills stood out against a sky of elusive and changing colours.

Above a green stretch of narrow *machair* land backing a strip of beach I saw a few cottages scattered among tiny fields won from the rocky outcrops by generations of crofters.   In between, the ground was much broken up by low bluffs and little woods of birch and hazel, bent and stunted where they faced the sea winds, dense on the inland side.   The air was fragrant with the scent of honeysuckle, mint and bog myrtle, and the tinkle of a little burn made melody.   Just the place to spend the night, I thought, for it was now rather late to pick my way down to the settlement to seek accommodation.   I often passed the night in the open when footloose among the hills.   So I found a sheltered nook under a low overhang where last year's leaves still lay in a thick dry drift and the rock still retained some of the day's heat.   I ate the last of my sandwiches, washed them down with a drink from the burn followed by a final pipe, then shook out my light sleeping bag and prepared to settle down for the night.

Now, I have gone to some length to emphasise just how normal and peaceful were the surroundings.   Normally, with the open air and exercise, I usually fall asleep at once; but not this time.   I had a strange feeling that something was wrong, something intangible, that brought an unnatural chill into my bones, psychological, not physical.   For a long time I tossed and turned, but as dusk settled I did manage to slip into an uneasy doze.

Some time later I started up, wide awake, chilled to the marrow and frankly scared.   I slipped out of my sleeping bag, pulled on my boots, gripped my stick and stepped out into the open, faintly lit by the last of the afterglow away in the north.   The whole atmosphere had changed.   The thin, cheerful note of the burn had changed into something discordant, like snarling voices and evil whisperings. Feeling it better for my peace of mind to seek out the unknown rather than to await its coming, I began to stumble round the foot of the bluff; but in the deep shadows I had taken only a few steps when I tripped over a hidden stone and pitched head first into the stony face of the cliff. However, instead of meeting stone, my outflung hands clawed through a mat of ferns that grew there in profusion and I overbalanced into some narrow opening behind. I was conscious of a black void — and if ever a place reeked of evil, that did.

I confess to being panic-stricken. Dragging myself back into the open, I stumbled back to my couch, where I flung everything into the sleeping bag, slung it over my shoulder, and made off. Tripping and falling, I splashed across the burn to the other bank — anything to get away from.....I know not what. But on the other bank, what a sudden feeling of relief came over me. It was like going through a gate into a fortress and shutting out pursuers on the other side. I am sure now they were supernatural ones: you remember how in *'Tam O' Shanter'* Burns described it in the simple line: *'A running stream they dare na cross.'* Suddenly I felt tired and relaxed, and lying down on a cushion of moss and heather I fell sound asleep. I was awakened by the morning sun shining through a gap in the hills above.

After a wash in the burn and a nibbled biscuit, I set off down to the houses by the shore. Crossing the burn, I had to pass close to the scene of my midnight episode, marked by a few crushed and broken ferns hanging on the seemingly solid face of rock. Although the sun was shining brightly by now and a thin mist rising from the hilltops giving promise of another fine day, the feeling of uneasiness came over me again as I stood there uncertainly. However, curiosity overcoming misgivings, I parted the ferns and pushed through. At first it was no more than a wide crack angling into the cliff, but it widened into a narrow gloomy cave with light filtering through a screen of scrub and coarse heather almost meeting over the long gap in the roof. A natural shelf of rock, crumbling in parts, extended below the overhanging face into the dark recesses.

When my eyes became adjusted to the dim light, the first things that caught my attention were scattered fragments of wood littering the shelf, which I found on taking a closer look were the rotted staves of small kegs or barrels. Beyond them lay rolls of some kind of fabric covered with flakes of stone and detritus. With my curiosity now thoroughly aroused, I lifted a corner of one of the rolls, but it came away in my fingers. Stained and rotten though it was, I could still see the lustre of what had been fine silk in the exposed layers.

I remembered then how this part of the west coast used to be one of the centres of smuggling, where cargoes of wines and silks and other luxuries from France were landed to cheer the households of the clan chiefs and leading families in this then inaccessible area. Surely this must be an old forgotten hoard. But why forgotten? What had happened to the operators long ago?

As I stood ruminating I noticed a jar of perhaps a gallon or so standing near the edge of the shelf beyond the rolls of material. As I stepped forward to examine it I saw with some interest that the stopper was intact and hammered well home; but at a touch the crumbling stone gave way below and the jar, slipping through my fingers, crashed on the rocky floor and split up the middle. It was maddening to see a small flood of liquid gold going to waste, filling the air with the bouquet of old brandy. However, I managed to save some of it trapped in one of the larger fragments and poured it into the little flask I carried in my haversack, which happened to be empty — nothing unusual! Now all this had distracted me from the repelling atmosphere of the place, but this returned in force as I began to move towards the inner and darker end of the cave. In fact, I found myself forcing one reluctant foot in front of the other. Just what was there about the place so fearsome and repelling?

I was just about to turn and leave when I saw the glint of some tiny object further along the shelf. Peering down, I tried it with tentative finger, and there under the film of dust, I saw two coins of yellow metal. Picking them up, I was about to take them back into the light for a closer examination, when my eyes were irresistibly drawn to something on the floor at my feet. It took me a few seconds to identify what was lying there, and when I did I started back petrified with horror. What I had at first dismised as a tangle of brown sticks and two round stones resolved itself into two human skeletons. The arms of the one were upraised, with the finger bones still partially fixed into the neck of the other, and between the ribs of the strangler was jammed the rusted blade of a long knife or dirk. The leg bones were covered up by a drift of leaves and mould and in among the bones lay rusted buckles and scraps of cloth and leather.

The horror of the place came surging back. The walls seemed to crush in. In my ears were the sounds of screams and curses. As I turned and rushed in terror towards the entrance my imagination flamed with the vision of the great horned goat-figure, with cloven hooves and fiery eyes, the embodiment of evil, that had made this cave its sanctuary. Laugh if you like. When I think back I feel ashamed of my panic and inflamed imagination — that is, if I DID imagine it. Anyway, I grabbed my gear, shot out of the cave and unashamedly took to my heels. Reassured presently by the serenity of the summer morning, and with the cave out of sight and far behind, I slowed to a halt panting and trembling with the effort.

The first thing I discovered was that I still clutched the two coins in my hand. They were apparently of gold, rather less than an inch in diameter and bearing the date 1721. Later I identified them as a pair of Louis d'Or of the type current in France about the middle of the eighteenth century. I tucked them away, hitched my haversack, took up my stick, and continued thoughtfully and more sedately towards the shore.

An hour later, sitting at breakfast with a hospitable crofter and his wife, I described — not the finding of the cave (I have kept that to myself until now) — but the strange fears that had come over me up there in the night. The man looked at me queerly. After I had described the exact place, he remarked that that was one place no local person would go near. No birds sang there, nor would the cattle graze on the lush grass growing beside the burn. He added that when he was a boy he remembered hearing the old folk speaking about a fight that took place somewhere near over treasure stolen from Prince Charlie, but neither the fighters nor the treasure was ever seen again. There was a *buidseachd* (curse) on the place. Thoughtfully I took the road again and the experience became no more than a grim memory.

But there is a remarkable follow-up to the incident. Some time later I was sitting by the fireside reading again the sad story of Prince Charlie, in particular the carefully recorded *Account of Charge and Discharge* kept by his Treasurer, George Murray of Broughton. When I came to the items debited against the sum of £30,000 in golden Louis d'Or brought over from France to finance the ill-fated expedition, certain words in the text seemed to leap out:

> '.....When the French ships were attacked at Borrow-dale.....the money was landed and secreted in a wood, lest the enemy prevailed and made a descent, and whilst it was there one of the casks was carried off by an Irishman.....and one D- - -l.....but finding they could not convey away the whole.....broke it open and took one bag, which upon reckoning the whole sum was found to have contained 700 Louis d'Or'.

The record went on to add that the two men had vanished, presumably fleeing from the district with the bag of gold.

Well that is what happened. I still have the Louis d'Or, of the kind circulating in Scotland during the Jacobite uprising; also the little flask of brandy I just cannot get round to tasting. There is the crofter's story and now this old record. Did I stumble literally on the solution of an old mystery? Does a small fortune in gold still lie under the bones of the two robbers and two centuries of drift on the floor of the cave?

Just don't ask me to test my theory by returning to the cave, or even ask me the location. For me, it is effectively walled in by evil, and I wouldn't enter it again, no, not if all the gold in France was lying there in sacks ready for the lifting.

WITCHES

AND

THE CAILEACH BHEUR

DRAGONS

THE CAILLEACH BHEUR

In days gone by, witches were feared, respected or consulted professionally in the Highlands and Islands. In the less enlightened south, they were lashed to a post and incinerated within a pile of faggots and what was left was interred at the cross-roads and pinned to the ground with a paling stob. Thus inspired, the virtuous and learned defenders of the public proceeded to 'smell out' more victims by methods reminiscent of Zulu witch doctors. By the way, they were not entirely unsympathetic to the witches. With due observation of their spiritual welfare, cross-roads were chosen as a burying place at a site as near to the sanctity of a churchyard as the clergy would allow — the sign of the cross, you see.

However, this is by the way. In the islands, while witches were given a wide berth, they were at least allowed the freedom of the community, and on occasions, for a consideration, they might be invited to help out with their specialised gifts, for instance, in bringing about the sinking of the Armada ship in Tobermory Bay, or delaying the birth of Alan na Sop.

Strangely enough, there are few records of warlocks or male witches. Seemingly the female of the species was more deadly than the male. In appearance they varied from fairy-size up to giantesses, although of course they could assume any form they pleased. They are not to be confused with the Little People, or Fairy Folk.

Of all the witches of the Hebrides, the Cailleach Bheur, closely associated with the Isle of Mull, was the most impressive, even if she had only one eye. She is more famous for the legends connected with her than for any acts of witchcraft. In fact, her personality is reflected in stories from Scandinavia, home of the Trolls, and Central Europe, land of witchcraft. Be that as it may, we are told she was so tall that when wading across the Sound of Mull, the water came barely to her knees. Her home was within a great natural enclosure of giant boulders that lies in the south-west of the Ross of Mull. She had lived over such a long period of time that her herds of cattle and deer once grazed on lands extending far to the south of Mull, gone long since through the action of Nature's agents of erosion and now covered by the sea. This ring of boulders reminds me of a similar natural enclosure at the Quiraing, in Skye, within which the giants of Fingal kept their sheep. They had the great dog Luath, which ran so fast that when it was guarding the sheep it circled the enclosure so speedily that the sheep thought there was a dog at every single opening.

The origin of Loch Awe is attributed to Cailleach Bheur. At the time she was staying on the Mull of Kintyre, and every morning she used to take a stroll away up to Ben Cruachan, to one particularly rich stretch of grass where she grazed a favourite cow. Nearby, on a shoulder of the Ben where she used to rest, there was a well of pure water covered by a huge slab of granite, which she removed to allow her cow to drink. Now, this well had magical properties, for if the slab were not replaced without fail between sunset and sunrise, the water might gush out in such a torrent that the world itself could be engulfed.

On this particular day the Cailleach uncovered the well as usual; but lulled by the warm sunshine and soft breezes she fell into a deep sleep. Sunset came, but she slept on. Then, just as the sun dipped below the distant purple hills, the waters of the well began to stir and gurgle and suddenly a great flood came pouring out, roaring down the mountainside and filling the glen below.

The noise effectively wakened the witch, and seeing what was happening, she snatched up her magic stick and uttered the appropriate incantations, whereupon the waters halted, and she dragged the slab securely across the well. Unfortunately, before she could do this, the long glen below had filled with water, and all her arts were unable to reverse the flow and empty it back into the well. Thus Loch Awe came into being.

Another time, when she was wading off the western shore, some earth and stones fell from the creel she was carrying on her back, and in this way the isles of the Hebrides were formed.

In spite of her seeming agelessness, the Cailleach ended her days in a surprisingly simple manner. Now, she grew old, just like everyone else; but on the morning of her 100th birthday she was able to restore her withered form instantly into that of a winsome girl simply by immersing herself in the magic waters of Loch Ba, in Mull. Thus her life would constantly be renewed. However, the success of this exercise depended on one condition — on the morning of her rejuvenation she had to ensure that her immersion took place before any living creature had awakened and uttered its first song or sound of the day.

On this, her very last day of life, the witch, now a tottering old hag, was hurrying down to the shore of Loch Ba, probably at the mouth of Glen Clachaig, where the fine gravelly beach invites a bathing expedition. She was later than usual — it would appear she was not a good timekeeper. This time, to her eternal misfortune, there came from the distance the restless bark of a shepherd's dog that halted her on the spot. Strive as she would, she felt rooted to the ground, just these few steps from the tantalising waters of Loch Ba. The last minutes of her life drained away and she sank lifeless to the ground as her last one hundred years ended.

I feel sorry for the Cailleach who appears to have been a reasonably benevolent witch who minded her own business. It is highly probable that a trial, conviction and disposal of this giantess would have presented an insoluble problem to one of the enlightened courts of the south.

CONSIDERED OPINION

The following story, which was reported in the Press some time ago, centres on the Island of Lewis (but it could well be any one of the Hebrides), where the lack of a civilised method of imbibing a small sensation or two has driven thirsty people into the 'Bothans' which are simply out-of-the-way huts where illegal drinking goes on, but which are subject to being raided by the police — although perhaps with an understandable reluctance. This time an Inspector was giving evidence in Court after a raid.

'When I examined the premises,' he began, referring to his notes, 'I discovered in one corner two pails containing 1,257 seals off beer cans. In another corner there was a case containing three empty whisky bottles, two half-full bottles and five unopened bottles, besides two bottles of brandy. There were thirty-one full cans of beer under the peats in the corner.'

Putting away his notebook he paused and addressed himself to the Sheriff:-

'After carefully considering the evidence from every angle, it is my own considered opinion that the place had been used for drinking.'

THE GALLEON AND THE FAIRY CATS

THE GALLEON
AND THE
FAIRY CATS

The witch that lived in Duart Castle was after all only a minor exponent of the Black Arts. In the islands there were such great names as the Cailleach Tiristeach (the Witch of Tiree), and the Cailleach a'Bheinn Mhòir (the witch of Islay), as well as the Tine Bheag of Tarbert, who specialised in controlling the wind and the sea. In Mull there was a namely practitioner called the Doiteach Muileach — not to be confused with the Cailleach Bheur, who was more a benevolent giantess who minded her own business. But greatest of all was the Suil Ghorm Mor, the Big Blue Eyed Witch of Lochaber, with whom this story concerns itself later on.

Now, if they still teach history in the schools, the Spanish Armada will not have been forgotten. Nearer home there is the well-known account of the storm-damaged galleon which took refuge in Tobermory Bay. We are told this was the *Florencia,* said to have been carrying a treasure in the form of the pay chests of the army of the Duke of Parma (which failed to set foot on English soil.) Driven right round the north of the British Isles on her way home to Spain and sorely battered by the storms, she anchored in the Bay a few hundred yards off what we now call the New Pier. She sank as the result of an internal explosion when about to depart.

Many attempts have been made to locate and recover the alleged treasure but with little recorded success. Less than 100 years after the sinking, when the tips of what was left of her upperworks still showed on the surface, Sacheravell, Governor of the Isle of Man, was present at salvage operations which are said to have had some success. If so, that would account for the lack of success of the many later expeditions. The riven timbers now lie deep in the hard silt under ten fathoms of water.

In 1588, Scotland was a neutral country, and every assistance was given by the Macleans of Duart to the Spaniards in the work of re-fitting the galleon and supplying provisions. In return, the Spaniards gave the services of 100 soldiers to assist the Macleans in an expedition over to Mingary Castle and among the Small Isles to pay off old scores against the MacDonalds and MacIans.

Three theories are offered to explain how the galleon came to be destroyed. The first submits that as the Spanish captain, Don Ferreira, refused to make adequate payment for materials and provisions, holding that the military services he had provided were sufficient, Maclean of Duart sent a relative on board to demand payment. He was seized and confined on board near the magazine. Finding that the ship was about to depart, in desperation he laid a train of powder to the magazine and blew up both himself and the ship.

Alternatively, the explosion was engineered by a spy, one Smollet, from Dumbarton, an emissary of Queen Elizabeth of England. But to me what is the only logical and acceptable theory is that the ship was overwhelmed and accidentally blown up by an army of fairy cats. It came about this way:

On board the galleon there was a Spanish princess, young and very beautiful as Spanish princesses always are in song and story. Now, for some time past she had had a regularly recurring dream which induced her to tolerate the hardships and dangers of the voyage. She dreamed of a long voyage by sea, at the end of which a handsome island prince was awaiting her. She could see him before her very eyes; but every time she was about to achieve the culmination of her dream she woke up — much to her disgust. Well, the young chief of Duart duly learned that there was this lovely princess on the grand ship in Tobermory Bay, so he called for his birlinn, and with a stout crew he rowed away up the Sound of Mull to welcome the strangers. It was purely a duty visit, he assured his wife.

No islesman ever looks bewildered or unsure of himself at his first sight of the great mysteries of the world, like his first galleon, or an early train, or the motor car, or even the aeroplane. So when Duart climbed on to the deck of this really magnificent ship, his easy and arrogant air indicated to onlookers that this was a sub-standard version of the much superior ships he kept at home. However, matters took a different turn when the princess, hearing strange voices, came up on deck to have a look. She halted — enraptured: here in the person of Duart was the prince of her dreams! The chief set eyes on her — and that was that. The duenna fled in righteous indignation, and they say nobody saw the couple on deck for a week afterwards.

This may have been the same Duart as involved himself with the daughter of Torloisk: certainly they do say there was only the one chief of the Macleans that ever stepped out of line. 'The MacDonalds,' it was always claimed 'were the warriors, but the Macleans were the gentlemanly fellows.' If it was the same Duart, it may be this chief and his scheming wife who are said to lie under the two recumbent slabs at the eastern corner outside the old chapel of Pennygown, being refused interment in the sacred ground within the walls. Be that as it may, the wife at Duart became aware of the proceedings on the galleon and determined to end them.

Obviously this would call for specialised witchcraft that would save her husband while eliminating the ship and the princess, so she

contacted the Doiteach Muileach. This practitioner was unsuccessful in her spells; so, too, were the other well-known witches,
whose mis-directed spells recoiled from the galleon and played
havoc instead with a passing galley of the MacDonalds, much to
their wrath and mystification. The witches got away with it by
explaining that it had something to do with the number of holy
silver crosses carried on the galleon.

Wrathful and frustrated, the Lady of Duart finally approached
the great Suil Ghorm Mor of Lochaber, who was quite optimistic
about her ability to clear up the matter. That night, assuming the
form of a scart (cormorant) she flew across to Tobermory, and up
there on the edge of the moors, within the dark shadows of the
Druid Stones, she cast her spells, calling up an army of cats, large,
fierce, red-eyed and brindled like their domesticated descendants
still to be found about the town. Under orders from the witch they
swam out to the galleon, clawed their way up the sides and set
about the crew, who had just been squaring away the yards and
heaving the anchor short for an early departure.

The terrified men went down under the teeth and claws of the
cats; every single one, except a seaman who fled down the ladders
with the cats hot on his heels; down into the magazine, where he
cowered in among the powder kegs. Here he was discovered by
the relentless cats. But as they leaped on him the brilliant sparks
off their fur ignited the loose powder: up it went, and with it the
magazine and the whole ship, which went down with the princess
and everyone on board. By the special dispensation of the witch,
Duart escaped and managed to reach the shore, and ultimately his
home at the castle. Perhaps when he was confronted by his wife
his one regret was that he failed to go down — or up — with the
ship!

THE DRAGON OF THE GLEN

THE DRAGON OF THE GLEN

Long ago, when there were many little kings in the land, a fearsome dragon made its lair on Cnoc Fhada, in Glenmore. It lived so long there that its body wore a hollow you can see to this day on the top of the ridge. Sheep and cattle vanished from the district, and Glenmore became a place to be avoided by man and beast.

The king was greatly embarrassed by the presence of this beast, so that in the end he offered the hand of his daughter in marriage and a share of his kingdom to any man who would rid him of this importunate dragon. Now, the king's daughter was very beautiful, and even without the monetary reward many famous nobles and fighting men were attracted by the proposition. Clad in armour and bristling with weapons they sought out the dragon, but the beast, becoming rather irritated by the growing scarcity of food, came leaping gleefully from its lair breathing fire and destruction, against which not even asbestos armour (and that had not been invented) would have been proof. Every challenger disappeared down its ravenous maw, until in the end no man would venture forth, and the king was in despair.

One day, however, a little ship dropped anchor at the head of Loch Scridain, at the west end of the glen, and some strange activities began. The crew unloaded a cargo of large empty casks which they lashed in a row to form a floating bridge between ship and shore. When it was completed, large projecting spikes were driven into the casks to form a kind of *chevaux de frise*. The whole project was the brain-child of a handsome but humble and impecunious young man who had sunk in it every penny he possessed.

Finally, when all was ready, a herd of cattle was landed: half-starved looking beasts, but they were all he could afford. If they could just keep their feet they would serve his purpose. Lightly clad and unarmed except for his *sgian dubh* or black knife, which he used to goad on the cattle, he began to urge them up the glen towards Loch Sguabain and the dragon's lair. Upon Cnoc Fhada the hungry beast scented the herd, and doubtless saying to itself — 'They'll never learn!' it came bounding eagerly down the hill breathing fire and smoke and with appropriate noises of gastric anticipation.

At once the young man turned the herd back on its tracks towards the ship — not that the cattle needed much urging when they saw the dragon. But when the cunning herdsman felt the fiery breath hot behind him he hastily killed one of the herd with his *sgian dubh* and kept pushing on the rest. The dragon halted just long enough to gulp down the dead cow, then took up the chase again, leaping and flying until once again it was close behind — whereupon another of the herd was sacrificed. And so it went on, one of the cattle being left to delay the dragon when the pursuit came too close. In fact, so well had the young man estimated his chances that he killed the very last cow right at the loch side, allowing him to dodge out to the ship between the spikes in the casks. The dragon, enraged by the threat of losing the last of its prey, began to drag its loathsome length along the casks towards the ship and the crew, who were now recoiling in terror from the bulwarks.

But all was well. First one spike, then another, began to connect with the anatomy of the dragon; the more it struggled, the more it impaled itself, until in the end, breathing a thin futile trickle of smoke, it was so immobilised that the young man was able to stroll out and dispatch it with ease.

Triumphantly the ship sailed away, towing behind it the line of casks bearing the tangible evidence of the success of the expedition, until it anchored in the bay off the township where the king lived.   Great was the rejoicing.   The handsome young man and the king's daughter fell in love with each other at sight, and the king was so delighted by the acquisition of such a fine and resourceful son-in-law that he turned the young man's abilities at once to managing the administration of the kingdom.   All lived happily ever after — if we except the greedy dragon and the unfortunate herd of cattle!

HISTORICAL TALES

THE BIG GLEN

THE BIG GLEN

The Glen More I mean is that bleak, rocky, wind-swept gash which cuts through the centre of the mountains of Mull, packing into its twelve miles more of interest and romance than any other Scottish glen I know. It begins at the little hamlet of Ardura, above the sea pool of the River Lussa which flows into sheltered Loch Spelve. On the mound above the cross-roads stands a tall square monument erected in the 1920s in memory of Dugald MacPhail — *Du'l da Strath Choil* — the bard of Mull, who composed that loveliest of Gaelic airs, which is the anthem of the island — *'The Isle of Mull'*. Four verses of the song are quoted on panels round the monument, which was built with stones carted from the birthplace of the bard away at Derrynaculan, at the western end of the glen.

There is now a new road extending from the car ferry at Craignure all the way to Iona. It is no anachronism where it passes through Glen More, which dwarfs and swallows it up. The traveller has time now to drive and look around, while on the old track care had to be taken all the time to keep to the road and avoid the ditches. At first it passes through woods of natural birch, holly and oak, with the Lussa flowing below, a fine little salmon river. The tall green carpet of Forestry plantations is beginning to take over. For instance, about two miles from Ardura, you have to leave the new road and struggle through the conifers to see the Pedlar's Pool where the Lussa cuts under a bluff below the old road. In fact, it is a lovely quiet walk from Ardura up the old road as far as the Pool, with the Lussa tumbling beside it.

This pedlar, or packman, after whom the Pool is named, came to a house in the Ross of Mull, as he was going his rounds, whose occupants had been smitten with the smallpox. Now, this loathsome disease, which lingered so long in the country, was regarded with almost superstitious horror by the people, and in this case, none of the neighbours was prepared to enter the house and care for the victims. Food and drink would be left at a safe distance outside to be collected, if the folk were able. It was left to the stranger, the pedlar, to take over the house and care for the invalids until the disease had run its course — whether they survived or not we do not know. Eventually, the pedlar shouldered his pack again and set out on his interrupted round. But one evening, as he arrived at this lovely spot beside the Lussa, he found that he had contracted so virulent an attack of the disease that he collapsed and died. They buried him there beside the pool, together with his pack, and you will see the spot marked by a substantial cairn surmounted by a simple iron Celtic cross inscribed: *'John Jones, died 1 April, 1891'*.

After another mile or two, the glen widens and becomes wilder and bleaker. Just beyond the ruined homestead of Torness *'The hillock by the waterfall'*, the great wall of Ben Talaidh (2496 feet) blocks the glen to the north, and the road swings west along Glen More proper. This is the mountain to which Sir Walter Scott refers in his *'Lady of the Lake'*, when he wrote:
'Sounds, too, had come in midnight blast
Of charging steed, careering fast
Along Ben Talla's shingly side
Where mortal horseman ne'er might ride.'
The ghostly horseman is Eoghann a'Chinn Bhig (Ewen of the Little Head), who haunts the roads of Mull after dusk, even flying out to Coll and Tiree; who rides madly round the ancient keep of Moy, Lochbuie, when a death is imminent in the family of MacLaine of Lochbuie.

Immediately below the ruined houses at Torness a path leads down to the ford over the Lussa and to the Falls, which lie below in a picturesque setting, where I have sat with an itching rod hand watching the salmon and seatrout circling the pool below the falls waiting for flood-water to allow them to ascend to the chain of little lochs above. I sometimes wonder if the 'leister' or salmon spear I possess which was recovered from the bed of a Mull river, would have been used on the Lussa, in the manner described in Dugald MacPhail's poetic references to the river.

On the way down to the ford and falls, about 200 yards below the lowest of the ruined houses to the left of the road, there is a little cairn sunk deeply in the heather. Thanks to the careful directions of the late Seton Gordon, that great lover of the Highlands and Islands, I was able to locate this exact spot, repair the cairn and perpetuate the story which would otherwise have been lost for ever; for this is where the headless corpse of Eoghann a'Chinn Bhig slipped off the back of his exhausted charger, and his faithful servants marked the place with a tiny cairn.

Ewen was son and heir to the 5th chief of Lochbuie (whose clan was descended from John Dubh Maclean, 4th chief of Duart). He was married to a greedy wife, daughter of MacDougall of Lorne, who nagged him unceasingly to take over more and more of his father's lands. However, the chief, feeling that enough was enough, at last flatly refused any further concessions. Torn between his father's refusal and his wife's nagging, Eoghann persisted in his demand; tempers flared, and in the end the matter could only be settled by the sword. So the old chief, with his brother the chief of Duart (who shrewdly joined in for the pickings) faced up to Eoghann and his followers.

In the old days clan fights used to be settled in a gentlemanly way — like duels — at a time and place mutually agreeable. I cannot find out exactly where the fight took place, but I believe the site is called Blar Cheann a'Chnocain somewhere between Loch Sguabain and Craig, further along the glen — '*A grassy lawn, where the bones of the dead victims have long mouldered to dust.*'

The evening before the fight, as Ewen was riding along on his black charger, he espied a fairy woman dressed in green washing blood-stained clothing in a little burn. Greeting her with due civility, he asked if she could tell him how the battle would go next day.

'Tomorrow morning,' she replied, 'If you find butter on the breakfast table, you will win; if it is not there and you have to ask for it, you will lose.'

Next morning, as he reached for the butter on the table, there was none, and he had to ask the serving girl to bring some. As he did so, the words of the fairy woman came back to him and filled him with misgivings. However, he prepared for battle, took up his arms, mounted his charger and set off to the appointed place.

As the tide of battle began to run against him in spite of his bravery, Ewen was caught at a sudden disadvantage by an opposing clansman, who with one mighty slice of his broadsword cut Ewen's head from his shoulders. The headless body, jammed in the stirrups, was carried from the battlefield by his maddened charger as far as the ford of Lussa, where, as I described, the body slipped out of the stirrups as the exhausted horse faced the steep hillside above the river. Tradition says that when the headless body was carried home and was seen by his favourite hunting hound, every hair on the dog's body turned white.

So there you have the story of the Headless Horseman; but mind you, confrontation with his ghost in these modern days has sometimes been blamed for certain traffic offences more closely associated with late closing hours and over-indulgence!

As an aside, I can also tell you about a twisted tree along by Loch Ba which was gripped as a young sapling by a Maclean clansman with one hand as he fought off the Headless Horseman with the other. The struggle went on from dusk to cock-crow, when, of course, the ghost had to retire to the shades: but the struggle had been so fierce the sapling was almost torn out the ground by the roots and survived as an old tree lying almost horizontal.

West of Torness the glen follows the southern perimeter of the great Ben More double volcano which was centred on the head of Loch Ba during the Tertiary period, 50/25 million years ago. Folding and crushing of the rocks left this line of weakness which was cut, gouged and smoothed finally by the glacier ice to form the valley. Today we see the floor of the glen littered with huge isolated boulders — erratics, they are called — left behind when the conveyor belt of ice melted and retreated. We see, too, numerous moraine mounds dropped when the glacier halted temporarily and released its load of stones and detritus as the face melted. Bare slabs of rock in the glen and along the seashore at its western end bear the gouges and scratches caused as the rocks embedded in the ice were dragged along.

As the glen levels out, the thin skin of earth is replaced in places by deep holes filled with peat which presented the contractors with construction problems when the road was being made. Two bulldozers were swallowed up in one such hole. However, the skin of grass supports a good stock of sheep and this is also a sporting area where the deer can range far from the Forestry fences and plantations, and come down in herds to the lower levels where grass is still to be had during the depths of winter.

We come now to a chain of three little lochs below the road curving round to the south towards the lands of Lochbuie. The nearest is Loch Sguabain, out of which flows the river Lussa, and in which you will see the crannog-fortress-island which was the home of Eoghann a'Chinn Bhig. Many stories are centred on this middle section of the glen, bleak and lonely, where hardly even a scrub willow bush grows. Above and to the south of the loch rises Ben Fhada (1603 feet) on the top of which is the long hollow where the dragon that terrorised the district once lived.

But rather more recent, reminding us of an incident in the days of the Fingalians — the Celtic giants of Ireland and parts of Scotland — you will see a huge pointed boulder half embedded in the soil beside a lay-by in the old road above Loch Sguabain.   There are only a few references to the presence on Mull of the Fingalians. Fingal's Cave in Staffa appears to have no connection with the great man himself, but only to fantasy.   There is a Fingal's Table in MacKinnon's Cave over at Gribun.   That is about all, except for the following:

One day the giant Nicol was standing on the shore of Loch Spelve, looking across the intervening hills at his fellow giant Sguabain, who was standing there.   Their verbal exchanges became heated to a point where Nicol, in a fit of petulance, tore out a huge boulder and hurled it at Sguabain.   Easily avoiding it, he in turn lifted an equally large rock and directed it at Nicol.   This stone can still be seen beside Loch Spelve, while Sguabain's Stone, as I described, lies beside the old road above the loch that bears his name.

Looking along the eastern slopes of Ben Buidhe, above Loch Airdeglas (the uppermost of the chain of little lochs), I always wonder who was the *sagairt*, the minister or missionary, to whom the place-names of burn, wood, spring, croft and hillock refer? There could be no more bleak or remote a corner of Mull for his cell.

Just beyond this romantic area we cross the watershed, where the mountains close in and the great purple mass of Ben More (3169 feet) dominates the north-west skyline.   The mountain mass holds the clouds when the rest of Mull is revelling in sunshine, and of course Glen More, in the cloud shadows, seems even more bleak and gloomy that it really is.

We come then to Craig, formerly a shepherd's house, now modernised, and the first inhabited house in the ten miles from Ardura.   There is a fine run down the straight new road, down the

225

widening glen with the distant spread of Loch Scridain. About a mile from the head of Loch Scridain you will see the walls of a sheep fank to the right of the road, with a notice directing the walker over the eight miles of right-of-way from Glen More to Loch na Keal at Knock and Loch Ba, crossing the 1100 feet watershed on the shoulder of Ben More at the head of Glen Clachaig, which leads down to Loch Ba; a hill walk I can thoroughly recommend.

Opposite the sheep fank, on the south side of the road, the path continues by the side of a hill burn and crosses a ford of the Coladoir River, which drains the west side of Glen More, as the Lussa does the eastern.

The Coladoir looks bare, bleak, clear and forbidding, running over a bed of bleached rocks and boulders with an occasional deep crystal-clear pool. I saw few if any fish of any size although I am told that further up it is a good fishing river.

A walk of under a mile along this path — an old cart track — takes one to the ruins of Derrynaculan, birthplace of Dugald MacPhail. It was a substantial house, with an upper storey, now in ruins, of course, and outside it is a small clump of very old trees — perhaps the *'Doire'* or wood after which the place is named. There is a big sheep fank behind, all backed by a deep cleft in the steep hill face down which a high waterfall descends like fine lace. An idyllic setting in good weather, with good fields running along beside a deep pool of the Coladoir; but a howling wilderness in winter when the Atlantic gales funnel unopposed through the glen, so much so that the telegraph poles had to be specially set and anchored to stand up to the conditions. One or two holly trees struggle along the Coladoir, blasted and whitened on their windward sides. No wonder Dugald MacPhail preferred the quiet beauty of Strath Coil at the other end of the glen.

We come back to civilisation, as it were, at the crossroads at the head of Loch Beg, which opens into Loch Scridain, not far from Kinloch Hotel and the start of the occasional farmhouses. To the right the road goes round Loch Scridain, to Loch na Keal and back to the Sound of Mull at Salen.   Our main road continues through the Ross of Mull to end up at Fionnphort, ferry port for Iona. ᴊehind us lies Glen More, barren of everything but its store of legends and traditions.

'LET THE TAIL GO WITH THE HIDE'

'LET THE TAIL
GO WITH THE HIDE'

That is a quotation still remembered in the island, and the story to which it applies is typical of the clan intrigues of the 16th century. It is a sequel to the death of Eoghann a'Chinn Bhig, whose father, the 5th chief of Lochbuie, was then left without an heir. His brother, Maclean of Duart, who had cunningly sided with Lochbuie against Eoghann, promptly stepped in and seized the whole of the unsettled lands of Lochbuie. He gave these to his own son and imprisoned the old chief of Lochbuie in the island fortress of Cairnburg Mor, in the Treshnish Islands off Mull, where he was to languish for the rest of his life.

In this lonely prison Lochbuie had no other companion than a housekeeper, a woman of the clan MacPhee. Once in a while, in order to keep an eye on the two prisoners, Duart sent a boat to the island with provisions. After two years, the men reported back to Duart after a visit that the woman was about to become a mother, which greatly perturbed Duart, for he was well aware that a son, even though illegitimate, would be the lawful heir to Lochbuie lands. Therefore a nurse was sent to the island, along with a doctor, with instructions to destroy the child, if it was a male. The nurse was more sympathetic to the cause of Lochbuie, and when in due course twins were born, a boy and a girl, she concealed the son and reported the birth of a daughter to the conscientious doctor, who in all sincerity returned to Duart and reported that the child had been a girl, which quite reassured the crafty chief. The nurse resourcefully managed to arrange for the boy to be conveyed to remote Glencannel, where he was brought up by a MacGillivray family. He was known as *Murachadh Gearr,* or Dumpy Murdoch, from his short, broad build.

The lands of Lochbuie remained for years in the hands of Duart, who was quite unaware that only ten miles away, Murdoch, the young heir, was growing to manhood. Although short in stature, he had the attributes of a leader of men, and in due course he crossed over to Ireland to broaden his knowledge and learn something about the arts of war. After wandering around for a time he was admitted to the household of the Earl of Antrim, and given the traditional hospitality of a year and day with no questions asked, the usual polite conditions of hospitality in those days. Murdoch employed his time usefully in military training and sporting activities, in which he excelled.

At the end of the year, the Earl, who had been much impressed by his guest, asked Murdoch just who he was and what he was doing over in Ireland. Murdoch related the whole story of his family misfortunes and of his ambitions to recapture the ancestral estates. The Earl promised Murdoch the utmost help in preparing a punitive expedition.

The young man, however, confident that once his presence was known he would have the full support of his clan, set out with only twelve companions, arriving at dusk at the steep headland guarding the approaches to the ancient castle of Moy. Anticipating the difficulties, the party had carried scaling ladders with them in the boat, and with these they were able to reach the top of the cliffs undetected. Before them lay the castle at the seaward edge of the plain of Magh.

But the castle was easily defended and could only be taken by subterfuge, so Murdoch took it on himself to spy out the land.

Nearing the castle he heard a woman singing to the cattle as she attended them, but as he crept past a stone rolled from under his foot and the startled woman gave a sudden exclamation of *'Dia leat a'Murchaidh'* (God be with you, Murdoch). Feeling he could safely talk to her he went up and asked who was this Murdoch to whom she had referred. He was, she said, the long-lost foster son she had once loved up in Glencannel. Murdoch recognised her then as the MacGillivray woman of his childhood, and identified himself by showing her a peculiar mark on his chest, by which, to her unspeakable delight, she recognised her foster son.

Murdoch explained the purpose of his presence there and asked if she would be prepared to help him to recover the lands of his forefathers, to which she readily agreed. After some thought, she suggested a plan. When the garrison was fast asleep, she said, the gate of the cattle pens near the castle should be opened. In there were the calves that had just been separated from their mothers, and when they came running out there would be great noise and confusion. This would arouse the garrison, who would come rushing out to restore order; whereupon Murdoch's men, who would be ready outside the narrow main door, would slay them one by one as they emerged.

But Murdoch, always considerate, said to his foster mother: 'But how will we be sparing your husband, seeing that we will not recognise him in the darkness?' — to which the woman replied in her unwavering devotion to Murdoch — *'Leig an t-urball leis a'Chraicionn'* — Let the tail go with the hide.

Murdoch returned to his men, who approved enthusiastically of his simple plan. First they had a meal, then at midnight, refreshed and rested, they crept up and took up their positions outside the castle door, leaving one of their number to open the gate of the cattle pen. Out poured the calves, calling for their mothers, who bellowed in response and came galloping in from the open fields to claim their offspring. The woman, who was waiting inside the castle, roused the garrison, who all unsuspecting came rushing out to meet their deaths under the swords of Murdoch's men, leaving the castle open and undefended.

However, Duart's son and his wife, undisturbed by the noise outside, remained sound asleep in an upper floor, and were left undisturbed until morning when Murdoch quietly entered their room and announced that he was the rightful owner, that the castle had been taken, and that he would give them safe conduct to Duart, a generous gesture they were in no position to refuse.

Duart was irritated and perplexed and uneasy when he heard the news. Who could this strange claimant be? Surely he could have trusted the word of his doctor when the birth of a girl was announced in the past: yet the only true claimant had to be a son. Old friends and clansmen rallied to Murdoch's cause and the true story of his secret birth and upbringing spread far and near, finally reaching the ears of Duart, who realised he had been duped.

Murdoch and Duart both gathered an army. With the estates of Lochbuie firmly in his hands, Murdoch advanced on Aros Castle, then a stronghold of the Macleans, and in the evening the two armies faced each other across the flat ground at the mouth of the Aros river.

One little incident took place involving the boldness of one of Murdoch's men. A poor old woman had given her only cow to provision Murdoch's army (she was given a herd of sixteen in its place later on). Lacking a proper cooking pot to prepare the meat, this man slipped across the shallow river and mixing with a party of the Duart men round a fire he calmly told them that they had had the use of the big cooking pot long enough, and others were waiting for it, and picking it up, he unhurriedly strolled away. Not until he was crossing the river did the Duart men realise how they had been hoodwinked and they sent a shower of arrows after him — which are said to have rattled like hail off the cooking pot, for the resourceful man had placed it over his head like a helmet!

Later in the night another secret sortie was made into the ranks of Duart's men, this time by Murdoch himself and his faithful lieutenant, an Irishman called MacCormick. Avoiding the sentries the two men crept right up to the place where Duart was lying asleep, still clad in his armour, and with his hand on the hilt of his broadsword, ready for the morning's battle. Murdoch, thinking with a heavy heart of the slaughter that would follow, and seeking to avert that rather than to carry out his vow to be avenged on Duart, gently slipped the sword out of his uncle's grasp and substituted his own, after which the two men returned safely to their own side of the river.

In the morning, when Duart awoke and discovered the exchange of broadswords, he knew Murdoch had spared him although at his mercy. Duart's heart smote him and he realised it was his greed and wounded pride that had brought the two clans so near a sanguinary battle. He disbanded his men and hastened to meet Murdoch. The outcome was a pact of friendship between Murdoch and his uncle that lasted all their lives, and thus Murdoch, the sixth chief, came into bloodless possession of his father's lands of Lochbuie. Murdoch died in 1586.

His faithful lieutenant was not forgotten. Murdoch directed that anyone of the name of MacCormick was to receive the hospitality of the castle of Moy, and on the lintel above the entrance he caused to be inscribed in the stonework: *'Biath agus Deoch do MhacCormig'* — Food and Drink to MacCormick.

AILEAN nan SOP

AILEAN NAN SOP

The name of Alan na Sop — Alan of the Straws — does not resound through the pages of history like such names as Donald Balloch or Angus Og, MacLeod of Dunvegan or Campbell of Argyll; even less like the MacDonalds of Islay, for a time Lords of the Isles and Earls of Ross. Perhaps Angus Og had the greatest affinity with Alan na Sop; he, too, was a proud and bloodthirsty leader, whose galleys vanquished the combined fleets of his uncle John, last Lord of the Isles, and the Macleans of Duart in the greatest naval battle in the Hebrides, where the sea ran red with blood, giving the name of 'Bloody Bay' to the scene of the battle off the north coast of Mull.

Of course, there was the great Col MacDonald of Islay, in the 17th century, the first Colkitto, whose son became the mighty general under Montrose. He was so called because of being left-handed. Colkitto's Galley became a name feared in every island of the Hebrides.

Alan na Sop was to become a thorough and calculating pirate. He had no need to paint his galley in different colours, like Clanranald or the raiding MacIans of Ardnamurchan, for he feared no man. He rose to be the inspired leader of fighting men who raided not only the southern Hebrides, but parts of the mainland and far down the Lowland coasts. He was fortunate in having influential friends in high places who protected him from the wrath of the distant Scottish Parliament. However, I am jumping ahead.

Alan na Sop, an illegitimate son of Lachlan Cattanach Maclean of Duart, was born to the daughter of Maclean of Torloisk, with whom Duart had been rather over-familiar during his visits there. The girl, degraded in the eyes of her family, was relegated to menial duties in the kitchen. The birth of her baby became overdue; days and then weeks passed, to the increasing discomfort of the poor girl.

One day a travelling tinker, in the kitchen at Torloisk House, asked the reason for the unhappy state of the girl. On being told the whole story he at once suspected the influence of witchcraft, and having learned something about the Duart household in the course of his rounds, he hit on an idea to break the spell. He suggested to the girl's father that word be sent secretly to the Chief of Duart of the birth of a boy; but care was to be taken by the messenger that the chief's jealous wife would 'accidentally' intercept the letter and learn the terms of the message. The wily tinker's plan worked like a a counter-charm. The Duart wife (who was doubly jealous, because she had no children of her own) flew into a rage when she learned the news, and rushing into the kitchen at Duart she tore a rusty key out of a bag hanging on the wall and hurled it into the face of the old witch, a member of the household staff, who had cast the spell on Torloisk's daughter.

The disturbance of the key broke the spell and at that very moment at Torloisk a boy was born so quickly that the servants had hardly time to spread a bundle of straw for his mother's accouchment in a corner of the kitchen. The boy's very first action was to grasp a handful of straw in his tiny fist, so all his life he was known as Alan of the Straws.

However fanciful the story of his birth, his life is fairly well recorded. He grew up to be a strong and agile boy with that dash of daring he was to develop to the full when he grew older. Unfortunately, when he was only a boy, his mother, now the sole remaining member of the family and as such highly eligible, marrried a member of the clan.   Alan's stepfather proved to be cruel and heartless, both to the boy and to his mother.

As an example of this there was the incident of the bannocks. There was nothing Alan loved more than oatmeal bannocks, and being a very early riser he used to bake a batch of them for himself every morning beside the blazing peat fire.   One morning his stepfather, pretending to help the boy pick up the scalding hot oatcakes, thrust them into the small eager hands and closed the boy's fingers on them.   His hands were so badly burnt that he bore the scars all his life.   Allan never forgot the incident, nor the manner in which the cruel man had mocked and laughed at the boy's screams of pain.

This boyhood persecution may have hastened the lad into the career of callous and reckless daring he was soon to take up.   As late as the 16th century Danish pirates still roved the high seas, raiding the western mainland and the Hebrides from time to time.   Attracted by the free seafaring life, Alan joined up with one of the pirate ships and so distinguished himself that in his early manhood he was already master of a ship.   From then his trade as a sea rover expanded until he commanded his own fleet, manned by crews who would follow him to the death.   His name became feared throughout the whole area.

Meanwhile, his stepfather, apprehensive of the power and influence of the young man whom he had so abused as a boy, feared a descent on Torloisk for the repayment of old scores: but when Alan's fleet did eventually anchor off his old home the man found that Alan's thoughts appeared to have risen above such matters as petty personal revenge.   Greatly relieved, the now old man welcomed and feasted his stepson and his men.

Not content with this, however, the old schemer began to play on Alan's feelings, hinting that he should settle down under the protection of his friends to enjoy the fruits of his plunderings. Why, he added, there lay the fine island of Ulva, complete with all the comforts a man could wish.

Why, it was the ideal place for him.   All he required to do was to eliminate the old MacQuarrie chief of Ulva and seize his lands.   Torloisk failed to mention that he had been scheming for years to get rid of the fine old chief, who had been an embarrassment to his plans for a long time.

The idea appealed to Alan and he set sail for Ulva across the loch with the plan in mind.   But when he landed, with his powerful fleet at his back, old MacQuarrie, though fearing the worst, assumed a bold and friendly front and hastened to the shore to welcome the pirates, expressing his pride in entertaining such a famous company.   Then as time went on Alan began to remember the few really happy days of his childhood, days he had spent over on Ulva as a guest of the same chief, and his heart began to warm again to the old man.   In fact, when he was preparing to leave, having dismissed his cruel plan, he confided frankly his original reason for coming.   MacQuarrie replied that a man like Alan could never have thought up such a scheme; it must have been planted in his mind by someone else.   Could it possibly have been his stepfather at Torloisk?

The young man shamefacedly admitted it, but with growing anger at so nearly have been made a tool of his stepfather.   He returned to Torloisk and confronted the old schemer.   Enraged beyond endurance, he threw the facts, his pent-up repressions, the perfidy, the cruel treatment of his mother, even the scars on his hands, into the face of this evil man, whom he then killed with a single thrust of his dirk.   Alan then decided to give up his piratical life and take over the lands of Torloisk, where he settled down and married, spending the rest of his life in the normal, if uneasy, life of an island chief.

A few stories of his later days are still told, for Alan was by no means a model of rectitude — he 'Could not behave in genteel society.'   One such tale, related to Seton Gordon by Robert McMorran of Treshnish (a storehouse of Mull memories) concerns the small fortress-island of Cairnburg Mor. Here at one place you will see a steep exposed shelf jutting out well below the lip of the cliff that encircles this flat-topped island. This is known as *Urraigh* (or *Leac) nan Ailean na Sop:* Alan's Shelf.

MacNeill of Barra and his very attractive daughter were paying a visit to Torloisk. One fine day Alan suggested they should visit Cairnburg Mor, so a galley was launched and the party duly landed on the rocky shore and climbed up the only access to the top.

Here Alan and the MacNeill's daughter became separated from the others, and he began to pester the girl with his attentions. Scared by his rough advances, she took to her heels along the edge of the cliff, but Alan caught up and clasped her in his arms. At that point a faithful servant of the MacNeills' who had witnessed it all came running up, tore the surprised man away from the girl and pushed him over the cliff edge before he could resist.

Fortunately for Alan, he landed on this *Urraigh* or projecting shelf a few feet below, where he could keep a precarious hold but was unable to climb up. Enraged as he was, but recognising his helplessness, he gave his word to the servant that if he gave him a hand up he would leave the girl alone and take no action against the servant for his presumptious act: whereupon he was helped back on to the top. The word *urraigh* is an interesting old Gaelic word indicating a sloping shelf, akin to the English *'eyrie'*.

It is said that Alan was the founder of the Torloisk branch of the Clan Maclean, but this is not supported by documentary evidence. He lived to a good old age and was laid to rest in St. Oran's Chapel, Iona, near the south end, where his piratical exploits are symbolised by a ship carved on his tombstone. He shares this ancient chapel (said to stand on the first site chosen by St. Columba to build a sacred edifice) with a distinguished company of saints and Christians dating back to St. Oran himself, who lies under a plain red stone next to the door. Some old Mull folk say Alan was interred in the old burial ground at Kilninian Church, and indeed

there are some very old and richly carved stones there that mark the
resting places of great people from the past.

ULVA'S ISLE AND DR. LIVINGSTONE

DAVID LIVINGSTONE
AND
ULVA'S ISLE

The great missionary-explorer Dr. David Livingstone was born in Blantyre; but while it is well known that his forefathers were connected with the island of Ulva, off Mull, few people know that they originally came from Ballachulish and still fewer that his grandfather was involved in the aftermath of the hanging of James of the Glen.   Still earlier, the family tree can be traced back to a Macleay who lived in the 15th century.

Now, the name 'Livingstone' is in the Gaelic *'Mac-an-Leigh,* or Son of the Physician, anglicised to Macleay.   The Macleays were descended from the famous Beaton doctors of Pennyghael, in Mull, physicians first to the Lords of the Isles, and then to the Macleans of Duart.   They were designated Royal Physicians after a visit to Edinburgh, where they so impressed the King that they were given that description, and also a grant of land.   Their skills, especially in herbal remedies, had been handed down by the monks of Iona.   A cairn commemmorating the two most famous of the Beatons stands beside the road a mile beyond Pennyghael in Mull.   It is surmounted by a plain cross bearing the initials — now nearly obliterated — *G M B 1582 D M B.*   The Beatons came originally from Bethune, in France, and hence the name, as well as the names of other descendants such as *MacBheathan,* anglicised to MacBeth or MacVean.

In fact, there were three families of Livingstones in the Appin area. One, in the days of Charles I, was given certain ecclesiastical appointments and settled in the old seat of the Bishops of Lismore.

Another family, in Benderloch, was once hereditary keeper of the Royal Forest of Dalness, at the head of Glen Etive. Members of this family became bodyguards to the Stewarts of Appin, with marriage connections, and one of those Livingstones saved the Stewart banner at Culloden and returned it to the chief at Ardshiel.

However, it is the third Livingstone family which concerns us, from which David Livingstone was directly descended, less distinguished in the past, perhaps, but of long lineage.

In the first half of the 15th century, two men were felling trees in Nether Lorne. A bitter quarrel started, ending by one of them, John Macleay, striking a blow at the other, a blow which proved fatal. Fearing drastic punishment, John fled and hid in the woods and caves, living on roots and whatever he could find. Some time later, he was cornered and captured by a Stewart hunting party; by that time he was more like a curious hairy animal than a human being. In fact he was nicknamed *Am Beathach Molach* or the Hairy Beast. He was taken back to a Stewart household, where he was made a servant and settled down happily when he found he was not to make atonement for his crime. He married one of the servant maids and lived for some time near Ballachulish, raising a family, until one day he was recognised by a friend of the man he had killed, who had sworn vengeance, and he who had been the Hairy Beast was slain on the spot.

However, eight generations of John Macleays followed him at Ballachulish. The ninth Macleay had five sons, Hugh, Neil, Donald, John and Angus. The ninth John, with Neil and Donald, followed their chief at Culloden, where the father was killed. By this time, the family name had been changed at some time and for some reason from Macleay to Livingstone.

But now to James of the Glen:

When Stewart of Ardsheil's estates were forfeited after the Jacobite uprising, his son, James Stewart, was living in Glen Duror, and he was *Seumas a'Ghlinne,* or James of the Glen. The estates were factored on behalf of the Commissioners of Forfeited Estates by Colin Campbell of Glenure, known as the Red Fox, although he was not actually a harsh man. In fact, he was friendly with James Stewart to a point where he was reproved by the Commissioners for undue leniency. (Glenure's mother was a Cameron of Lochaber, a family friendly with the Stewarts.)

However, as you can read in *Kidnapped* and *Catriona*, the Red Fox was shot at and killed in the wood of Lettermore by an unknown person — at least, one whose name has never been publicly revealed. In the absence of any likely culprit, James Stewart, although not near the scene of the crime at the time, and in any case friendly with the dead man, was apprehended and conveyed to Inveraray for trial. Word was conveyed to him secretly that a rescue attempt would be made on the journey, but James, confident in the outcome of his innocence, refused the offer. He is said to have known who fired the shot, but would not reveal the name of the man. This man himself had to be tied up in his own house to prevent his confessing to the crime as soon as he learned that James Stewart had been accused and was prepared to take the blame.

Alas for the hopes of James of the Glen. Before a prejudiced Campbell judge and Court the outcome was inevitable. James was sentenced to death by hanging, and on 7th November 1752 he was hanged from a gibbet set up above where the road bridge now crosses Loch Leven. Under strict military guard the body was left hanging, wired together as it fell apart, until by 1756 only the bones swung from the gibbet.

Disgusted by this unChristian degrading of the remains of a brave man, the three Livingstone brothers, Neil, Donald and John had a secret discussion on how best the bones could be removed for decent burial. Accordingly, one evening at dusk, Neil — Niall Mor, as he is often called — and Donald concealed a rowing boat on the shore at Lettermore just below the present hotel. Taking with them the necessary tools, they settled down within sight of the gibbet. In the meantime, John, the third brother, ostensibly out for a stroll, began to chat with the bored sentry, and after a while suggested that they should both adjourn to the nearby inn for a drink. Glad to relieve the tedium, for hardly anyone passed near the scene of the hanging, the sentry readily agreed.

They were hardly out of sight than the two brothers slipped out of hiding. They tore up the gibbet and carried it down to the boat, and also, with due reverence, the bones of James of the Glen. The tide was running so strongly in the narrows that they were unable to reach their destination, St. Munde's Islet, but landed instead on Eilean-na-h'Iubhraca, where the last remains of James of the Glen were laid to rest in a grave dug in the grassy hollow that lay between the rocky knolls at each end of the island. The bones may have been moved later to the Church, and a small brass tablet was affixed on the inner wall of Old Duror Church. The gibbet, which they flung into the sea, was washed up below Clovullen, on a spit of land still called Rudha na Croich, 'Point of the Gibbet.'

Knowing that they would be chief suspects, and that for such a flouting of authority there would be dire and vindictive punishment, Neil and Donald left the district at once and rowed down Loch Linnhe to Morvern. We do not know what happened to the third brother, but doubtless he, too, would not be be slow to disappear. Feeling that Morvern was still too near Appin, they crossed over to Mull and ended on the fertile island of Ulva, off the west coast.

Here they took over a croft and in due course Neil married a Mary Morrison and Donald a Mary Beaton. When the croft became too small to support their growing families, Donald — with the threat of retribution now much faded — went back to Morvern and settled there. Neil remained in Ulva. He was at Leittermore in 1776-77, and at Am Uamh in 1779-83. Then in 1788 he was at Fearrann-an-Ardairigh. Nial Bheag (Little Neil), who was to become the father of David Livingstone, was born and baptised there.

However, in 1792, there came a dispute with the factor following a false accusation laid against old Neil by a neighbour who had his eye on Neil's croft. He was ordered to vacate the land at the next term, and was so arranging when one day the factor called on him and (as apologetically as any such dignified person could) admitted that he had learned the true facts and that of course Niall Mor could retain his tenancy.

Neil, his pride cut to the quick by the whole affair, told the factor that he '.....*could never live under a man who would believe a defamatory story against me, and condemn me without as much as hearing my defence.....I am ready to go, and go I will.*'

Niall Mor, much respected in the Ulva community, arrived in Glasgow carrying with him the most excellent references. Later the family moved to Blantyre, where they found permanent employment. There his son Niall Bheag married Agnes Hunter, a woman of sound Covenanting stock. Their second son, David, who was to become one of the nation's great men, was born there on 19th March 1813.

David's life was a tribute to the loyal traditions of his forefathers, and he had all the integrity and strength of character inherent in his Celtic-Highland heritage.

THE LOBSTER

FISHERMAN

ALICK BAN

I have picked Alick Ban as a typical islander, one of the last surviving members of two old families of fisherfolk, the Mac-Dougalls of Haunn. The thatched houses there where the families used to live are now either in ruins, or restored as holiday houses. In front lie the green fields where their crops were grown and their cattle and sheep grazed. Just under a mile distant, down an old cart track that skirts the low cliffs, lies the inlet in the black rocks from which they sailed in their boats, open boats then, which were drawn up here for the last time, now gone with hardly a trace. The shed where they stored their nets and gear was flattened long ago by the Atlantic gales. This wild coast, facing the open Atlantic, with arresting views towards the distant islands, is avoided by shipping.

This was the background against which Alick Ban lived his life: the sea in all its moods. His first words on going out of a house were never 'What's the weather like?', but always 'How's the tide?' His brothers and cousins were all tall, powerful men. There were no engines in the boats in the old days, just unremitting toil at the oars, or the benefits of a scrap of sail if the wind was right. They fished for their household needs at first, then with improving communications, the sale of lobsters became profitable, and they began to specialise. Alick was one of the most knowledge-able lobster fishers in the whole area, and knew every nook and cranny of the coast within ten miles of his base.

It was during the 1920s that Alick Ban, out with his cousin Alick Breac (Freckled), landed one of the biggest lobsters ever recorded in the Western Isles. It was taken in the middle of Calgary Bay, off Craig a'Chaisteal. Far too big to get into the creel through the opening, but too greedy to let go, it was raised to the surface still gripping the creel, and there Alick quickly passed a rope round it. That lobster measured three feet and one inch from tail to tips of feelers, with a span across its extended claws of two feet and ten inches; the claws had a circumference of thirteen inches. Fourteen pounds in weight, it was sold for £5 to a leading Glasgow fishmonger, who had its shell on show in his window for months.

After his wife died and his son went away to work on the mainland, Alick lived at Quinish, where there was a fine natural anchorage beside a jetty formed by a wide, basaltic dyke. Here he had a shed to stow his gear and a few yards away a cosy little two-roomed house with a corrugated iron roof tucked snugly against a rocky outcrop. Although he had three miles to walk into the village of Dervaig, the road took him past the houses of friends and relations and he never found it lonesome. For some years he worked in partnership with his brother John. Latterly he limited his activities to the coast nearest his base; but always the quality of his catch was well-known. In fact, he had a firm order from the Cunard Line to supply the 'Queens' with all the lobsters he could provide. The high value of his catches afforded a good living, even from his restricted activities.

He was an exceptionally powerful man with wrists as thick as his forearms. He suffered a severe disability although he never complained. Serving in the Navy during the 1914-18 war on the battle cruiser 'Inflexible', he had the misfortune to fall from the rigging, landing with his thigh across the rail, then falling overboard. If he had struck the deck he would have been killed instantly. Now Alick, like so many fishermen, was unable to swim, but he could float, and for some reason did so in a perfectly upright position; and thus they found him nearly three miles astern by the time the great ship had been turned back to search for him. Although they saved his leg, it was shortened by a couple of inches and left him with a permanent limp.

His strength and resilience earned him the name of the Rubber Man. One night in a Portsmouth bar, Alick saw one of his shipmates being severely handled by a big group of sailors from a rival ship. Although normally the most inoffensive of men, this was too much for him; so he sailed into the fracas, shrugged off mass attacks like a tank and in the end left the floor littered with a dozen sailors wondering what had hit them while Alick and his shipmate calmly strolled away.

Knowing every inch of the coast and countryside, he could reel off the name of every burn, hillock and landmark, its history and names of the people associated with it. He could tell you about the great still — a miniature distillery — operated at one time by his forefathers in the cave under the cliff below Glacgugairidh. The Treshnish Islands, with their difficult landings, caves, forts, rocks, traditions and rare springs of fresh water — he knew them all. Over his lifetime he watched the vertical crack in the big square rock between Croig and Caliach that he called *Dun a'Bhan* widen, until the rock separated into two pieces. He could tell you about the isolated Caliach Rock at the headland, how it seemed to become more shapeless over the years. The rock itself was called after the old woman who climbed up the cliff there after being cut off by the tide. She became so smug in attributing her climbing success to her own cleverness instead of to Providence, Whom she should have been thanking, that as a punishment she later fell to her death on the rocks below.

It was an unforgettable experience to accompany Alick in his lobster boat, a ship's converted lifeboat driven by a twin cylinder Kelvin engine, doing his round of the lobster creels. I can see him yet, sitting in the stern wearing his inevitable battered, salt-stained soft hat, the tiller loosely held under his oxter, as he ground down between his palms a fill of strong tobacco for his stumpy pipe. We threaded our way among outlying skerries and fangs of black rock with the breaking swells spouting white around us coming in from the open Atlantic, lifting us high, then creaming for ten feet down the sheer face of the towering cliff just a few yards inshore, with the screaming of seabirds and the scent of the salty seaweeds. Down below in the clean cold depths, the great beds of kelp — the Tangle o'the Isles — swung slowly with the currents.

I never tired of seeing the strange assortment of sea creatures brought up in the creels. Sometimes there were giant whelks the size of a clenched fist. These, said Alick, were the grim cause of the non-appearance of the bodies of people who had been drowned in the Sound Of Mull. Great colonies of these whelks fastened on the body and weighted it down until only the bones remained. Once a vicious four foot conger eel forced its way through the stout hazel frame of a creel, but having cleaned up the bait, it could not lever its way back out again. Alick's sheath knife, used with respect for the vicious teeth, finished off the conger, and still squirming it was tossed into the well at the stern, that odoriferous corner where the bait was stored.

Here, in the deep water close against the cliffs, he showed me where the hull of the liner *Aurania* is lying. Damaged by enemy action off Islay in 1916, and abandoned, slowly sinking, she still drifted all the way to Caliach Point before she finally went down. Knowing exactly how she lay, Alick was able to direct salvage operations later carried out to recover the ship's safe and other valuables. 'And if anybody laughs if you tell them that a live lobster can be red in colour, tell them there are plenty of red ones down here in the rusting hull. They take on the colour of the place they are hiding in.'

I asked him what was the most dangerous experience he could remember. He admitted there had been one occasion when John and himself had been perhaps a little worried. This day they had been out at the Treshnish Islands. In spite of their weather lore they cut it rather fine in leaving to come home, for the wind suddenly backed and blew up a full gale that caught them in the open sea. It was impossible to turn back into the teeth of the wind and rising waves. John crouched over the engine casing with his hand on the throttle, ready to ease off when the stern kicked up and the propellor raced, clear of the water. He had to keep the engine going flat out when possible, the only way to avoid being swamped by the high, curling, overtaking seas. Alick stood braced in the stern gripping the tiller and meeting the thrust of each wave.

At last, with the engine running red-hot, they came racing through showers of spray across the tide-rip of Caliach Point and into the lee of the headland. They were hardly level with Dun a'Bhan when there came an unholy crash from the engine as a piston smashed and a connecting rod came out through the crankcase: yet the sturdy engine clattered and clanked along on the remaining cylinder, pumping seawater instead of oil, driving the boat almost the remaining mile to Quinish, where it seized solid just 200 yards off their jetty — and as Alick said, 'John and me just pulled her in with the oars in a few minutes. Yes, we were a bit lucky that time.'

There was another time Alick and his brother were returning home and were off Treshnish Point when the timing pinion in the magneto stripped, and the boat, with its engine out of action, began to drift inshore towards the rocks and reefs spouting white with the Atlantic rollers under the black cliffs. Now, Alick was no engineer — he was a man of the oars and the sails. However, they had an idea of what had gone wrong, and managed to feed a piece of stiff tarry twine between the offending timing pinions. By a miracle, when they cranked the engine — and the cliffs were dangerously close — not only did the twine take up the clearance and turn the magneto, but by a 1000 to 1 chance the timing was perfect, and the engine fired. In fact, they carried on for a fortnight with this makeshift device!

But there was another side to Alick's character. Although quiet and retiring, happier in the Gaelic tongue than in the English, on occasions, especially if he had had a dram or two, he would reveal himself as a fine Gaelic scholar, possessing a great store of traditional songs and stories handed down for generations. This could have been a valuable addition to the records of the Celtic Society but for a thoughtless act on the part of two people who should have known better.

One evening two people called in with a tape recorder at the house of a close friend, where Alick was spending the evening. He was in extra good form and was easily persuaded to sing some of his songs and relate a few stories, which he did with appropriate interjections. Poor Alick did not know that the tape recorder had been switched on all the time, and later on, against the quiet advice of the man of the house, they played it all back; and if their intentions were innocent, the outcome was tragic. When Alick heard himself on the tape, with the background of tittering and laughing, his pride was sorely hurt, for he thought they had been trying to make a fool of him. Deeply insulted, he rose and stalked out of the house, and from that minute he refused to commit his wonderful store of knowledge to tape for anyone, however, well sponsored. It all died with him in 1961.

I cannot leave the story of Alick Ban without relating an experience of his during the 1939-45 war, the period when he was living on his own at Quinish. Many a drifting mine, broken loose from its moorings in the great minefields among the Hebrides, was washed up on the rocky coasts and exploded with a rumble that echoed far across the wind-swept moorlands. This experience brings out his expertise that made handling a boat seem so deceptively casual.

This morning, Alick described how about five or six o'clock, when he came out to check over his gear for the day's work and an early tide, he was alarmed to see a mine drifting in with the tide no more than fifty or sixty yards from his little jetty.   He knew that if it carried on it would explode right in front of his house, which would be the end of it, his boat, and all his possessions.   So he got a bar of pig-iron kept for ballast, lashed on to it a few fathoms of rope, and put it in the stern of the little dinghy he kept tied up at the jetty.   A few strokes of the oars took him out to the mine.   Then he carefully leaned out and got a grip of two of the horns — not near the points, he assured me — and turned it over until he saw a ringbolt.   He tied the end of the rope to that and gently pushed the mine away.   Then he rowed out for some distance, towing the mine to deeper water where there was plenty of room, and tossed over the pig-iron for an anchor.   The he rowed in and had his breakfast.

'Later on,' he added, 'I walked into Dervaig and telephoned the Mine Disposal people.   They were there in their lorry nearly as fast as I got home myself.   Man, I wouldn't have their job!   When they were making the mine safe I was half a mile away behind a rock with my hands over my ears afraid to look!'

Alick is no more.   We just have the memory of this fine man of the islands and of his fascinating tales of things and people of the past.   We are all the poorer for his going, and we shall not see his like again.

TAIL PIECE

PHEASANT WITH THE WIND UP

A PHEASANT WITH THE WIND UP

Archie was an inveterate poacher, as knowledgeable in the ways of the keeper as he was with game.   He was respected by the keeper with an attitude of armed neutrality, for he knew Archie poached for the pot and nothing else.   However, duty was duty, and after missing a few pheasants, the keeper decided to catch Archie out.   Taking a newly killed pheasant, he set it up most realistically on a branch in the wood in a natural roosting place.   Then he retired to a comfortable hiding place and watched for Archie, who usually came locating the birds before he returned to snare them with a loop at the end of a long pole.

Right enough, along came Archie, who spotted the pheasant, paused below it, then walked on.   Waiting until he returned, the keeper saw Archie stop again, study the bird, and again move on.   The bird was still there next day just as the keeper had set it up.

A few evenings later they met in the bar, and over their drinks the keeper put it frankly to Archie: 'Now, chust between you and me — and it will go no further.   Tell me what you saw wrong about that pheasant I set up for you in the wood.'   In the same spirit Archie answered: 'Ach, man, did you effer see a pheasant sitting with its tail to the wind instead of its beak?'